Mindsamaze

3

Hodgson Press

Front cover designed by Nicole Smith

Title pages designed by Nicole Smith

Many thanks to Berni Lowe for proof-reading
and typesetting this edition of 'Mindsamaze'

Mindsamaze
3

An anthology of the best writing by the pupils of St Edmund's Catholic School, Portsmouth, July 2008.

First published in Great Britain by Hodgson Press 2008
Hodgson Press
PO BOX 903ᴬ
Kingston upon Thames
Surrey
KT1 9LY
United Kingdom
enquiries@hodgsonpress.co.uk
www.hodgsonpress.co.uk

ISBN: 978-1-906164-03-4

Printed in Great Britain by Lightning Source Ltd.
Typesetting and layout by Bernard Lowe

Mindsamaze

The Best Writing

The best writing, according to the criteria used by the judges of one of the most famous national creative writing competitions.....

"creates reality as well as observes it;

draws the reader right into the depths of the author's invention;

possesses magic, transformations, surprises, bounces on trampolines while juggling lobsters;

has a message, a philosophy of life, a vision of an alternative world;

like streakers amazes by its naked verve and speed;

has sensuous intelligence – can be smelt, felt, tasted."

List of Contributors

Contents

Cries from the Heart Darfur

Life

Oranges and Lemons

Remembrance

Short Stories

Dramatic Monologues

War

The Crucible

Inspired by Shakespeare

Imagine

Cries from the Heart
Darfur

The Choice of Life

Her legs are weary, her feet blistered, her eyes empty, her arms heavy with the weight of her lifeless baby.

"Mama, come here," I call out to her, but she doesn't hear me. Her ears are deafened by the sounds of suffering. People dying, babies crying, women's defenceless cries as heartless savages ravage them time and time again. "Mama, your baby is dead," I say.

She needs to leave the baby behind, or it will slow us down. Better we leave the child in an unmarked grave and live another day, than to carry it with us, then die on our way to the next refugee camp.

Mama looks at me for the first time since we left Darfur to come to Chad, and I can hardly hear her as she mumbles, "I thank God that Keke is dead; now my baby can rest. She can't feel the pain anymore."

Keke's face is soft, almost peaceful, as though she is fast asleep, but Mama and I both know that we will never see those big, brown eyes open again, those chubby cheeks dimple as she smiles, her cute little body float, as she runs to give us a hug. No, Keke is gone forever.

I can recall the days before her death and the panic we all felt, as we gathered our belongings in a hurry, knowing fully well that at any moment, one of the many rebel groups could attack our camp.

Mezi was huddled in a corner, weeping, because she had been gang-raped. "They were dressed like the police," she whispered, through her swollen lips. "I trusted them. Not only because they were the police, but also because they were men. Men are supposed to protect, not destroy."

My heart broke for her; I felt it shatter into millions of tiny, little pieces – connected only by the intense sorrow they each collectively contained. "Mezi, you have to get up," I said, as gently as I could. "We have to go now! They can come at any time!"

Mezi looked up at me for the first time since her rape, and I had to look away, for the vacancy in her eyes was too disturbing to bear. The expression on her face blank, she accepted her fate: "Either way, I'm dead. If the Janjaweed find us, they will kill us; if my family finds me first, they will kill me too. They want me dead, because I am a disgrace to them, now that I am defiled. We both know they will hunt me down until I am dead, so that I cannot be a shame to them any longer." A solitary tear escaped her eye and I watched it travel down her bruised face, as she acknowledged, "I'd rather be tortured and killed by evil men who despise me for my ethnicity, than die at the hands of my own flesh and blood for a brutality that I had no control over! Nothing that the Janjaweed could do to me now, will even come close to the torment of being murdered by your own father and brothers!"

We eventually had to leave Mezi behind; she refused to come with us and Mama and I had Keke to think of. As soon as we got to Chad, we'd be able to get her the proper medical attention that she needed. As we scaled monstrous hills and travelled barefoot across the scorching desert, I wondered if we would ever make it to our destination alive. "Let me hold her for a while," I said to Mama, holding out my hands to collect the unconscious child.

Keke felt like a dead weight in my arms, after only holding her for a few minutes, and I couldn't help but wonder how Mama had been able to carry her this whole way. I glanced down at her face and my heart bled, as I remembered the happy, energetic girl she once was.

While she used to be full of life and vitality, she was now weak and lethargic. While her eyes were once huge and bright, they were now sunken and blank. While her little body was once animated and healthy, she was now emaciated and plagued with disease. She was red and feverish, her eyes occasionally fluttering open, as though she was desperately attempting to look up at me. Her lips twitched, and she made some gurgling sounds, as though she was trying to speak. 'Oh dear God, please don't let her die!' I silently prayed.

We travelled for miles and miles, only resting when we got to camps that had been set up by other displaced people also on their way to Chad. The stories we were told – of corruption, murder, rape, torture, infanticide and mass destruction, all at the hands of the rebel groups, will forever be engraved in my mind. Even more distressing, were the news that reached us of Mezi's death. It was the Janjaweed that found her, before her family did. They couldn't cause her any more agony, for they found her dead. She had hung *herself, truly, sold herself to the devil.*

My depressing thoughts were disturbed by the sound of someone's baby crying, which then made me think about Keke.   I was determined that she wasn't going to die; she would recover and fill our life with joy and fulfilment once again.   Mama and I had suffered enough: losing our home, breathing in the foul stench of death, struggling to survive each day, each hour, each second. We wouldn't cope if we were to lose Keke – she was the light of our world, and life would cease to exist without her in it.

No one has ever been as anxious or as terrified as I was that night. Keke wasn't eating or drinking and her breathing was laboured and heavy; I knew she was struggling to breath. "Keke, Keke?" I called to her, hoping that she could hear me.

With any ounce of strength she had remaining, Keke managed to slightly open her eyes. She looked at me and in those big, brown pools swimming with tears, there was a silent farewell. I had my answer, and as her eyes shut, I knew deep down, that they would never open again.

Mama and I stayed by Keke's side for the whole night, taking turns holding her, so that when her little soul passed away, she would feel as safe and secure as she possibly could in a war-torn civilisation. It happened so quickly that it was over in an instant: Keke took one long gasp of air – her last breath – and then she was still, unmoving, lifeless.

Mama let out a heart-wrenching scream, as she sat on the dirt, cradling her dead baby. Tears streamed down her hollow face, and as I collapsed at her feet, together, we mourned the little angel that had left us too soon.

I snap back into reality and realize that as I was recalling the past few days, I was crying tears of release. Finally, I can let go and deal with all the trauma that I have been in denial about for so long. I watch Mama lay down Keke's cold body onto a blanket, and cover her little body with a soft cloth soaked in lavender. "Goodbye, my angel," Mama whispers, kissing her child's face.

"Goodbye, Keke," I say, tears I had retained for so long, finally flowing freely. I look at Mama and ask, "Do you hate them – the Janjaweed? If

5

not for them, there wouldn't be all this suffering, and Keke might still be alive!"

Mama stands up and looking off into the distance toward Chad's civilisation, there is a thoughtful expression on her face. She turns to me and replies, "No, baby, I don't hate them; I can't hate them. Although every fibre of my being wants to, I refuse to give them that satisfaction. Hate consumes and destroys, and where there is hate, there can be no love, and with no love, there can be no life. No, I choose to live – for me, for you, for Keke and for all the people back home in Darfur who continue to suffer each day at the hands of their own government. I choose to live..."

Khono Mtetwa

This piece won the Human Rights Watch Writing Competition, June 2008.

Darfur

Darfur is a region in western Sudan, bordering the Central African Republic. In an Arab-dominated country, the population of Darfur is mostly black African. For years, there have been tensions between the Arab herders and African farmers, who have competed for land gain and land possession. One would expect the government to be unbiased and attempt to restore a balance of peace and justice, while maintaining an ambience and reality of freedom and equality, but most shockingly, this is not the case. As a matter of fact, the system in Darfur is quite the contrary. Opposition groups in Darfur acknowledge that the government neglects their province and discriminates against the black Sudanese, in favour of the Arab community.

The conflict in Darfur began in 2003, when rebel groups began attacking government targets. In retaliation, the government launched a military and police campaign intent on eradicating the black Africans living in Darfur. As a result, more than 2 million people have fled their homes. The apparent mission of the Sudanese government is to forcefully and brutally drive the black Africans out of Darfur. Since 2003, over 200 000 people have been killed in the Darfur region and more than 2 million people displaced. However, I consider these statistics to be mere estimates, as the Darfurians who are murdered and driven out of their homes are nameless victims, who not only die and get victimized without any dignity, but also seem to be concealed in the government's veil of secrecy and mystery. Violence against civilians is prevalent – much of it targeted against women, who are gang-raped and although, thereafter, often killed, are most likely to be subjected to a lifetime of fear, humiliation, desecration and immeasurable shame.

Words are overestimated as bearing the capacity to express the magnitude of the suffering that others are forced to endure, when in actuality, the only individuals who know what life is truly like in Darfur, are the Darfurians who are experiencing it day after day. Therefore, no written text, word of mouth, or any gathered statistic can possibly disclose the unimaginable tribulations that are a factor of life for the innocent civilians living in Darfur.

The query that is prevalent in the minds of the adults living all over the world is: "Why is the situation in Darfur a matter of importance to people worldwide?"

My response is: "How can it not be?"

Nobody deserves to live in an environment filled with peril and occupied with fear. In fact, the most fundamental human right of all, that also happens to be the most essential, is safety and security. Doesn't everybody deserve to feel safe and secure and live a life of ease, wherein fear of being harmed is nonexistent? Doesn't every human being deserve to walk down the street and admire a beautiful day, without the fear of who may be out there in the concealment of the bushes – watching them, stalking them, preying on them? Surely, one human being's life does not have a greater value than that of another. Surely, we are all born as equals and the endurance of an individual should not be pushed to its limits. However, even at this very moment, countless men, women and children in Darfur, are huddling together in desolation, petrified of their own government, which has allied with rebel groups, intent on maintaining what some consider to be 'the worst humanitarian crisis of all time'.

To every outsider looking in on the events unfolding in Darfur, it is blatantly obvious that law and order in the region, is now completely nonexistent. How can law and order be considered present in a civilisation wherein women are candidly gang-raped, and along with having to survive and cope with the trauma of their ordeal, are also in a position wherein they have to fear being murdered by their own family – who view their rape as a great shame and disgrace, instead of as a brutal violation against their loved one? How can law and order be prevalent in a society wherein civilians cannot even trust their own police officials, as many members of rebel groups – such as the Janjaweed – disguise themselves as policemen, while other actual police officers have abandoned their duty to their people, in order to join in on the victimisation of innocent civilians.

The people living in Darfur have been abandoned and betrayed by their own government – the system that they thought they could trust and rely on. If the world were to avert its gaze and focus on its own individual countries, with their own separate affairs, then we'd also be committing a great injustice, as we'd turning our backs on all the helpless Darfurians in Sudan, who are crying out for some help and some intervention from the rest of the world.

In my opinion, the solution to ending the crisis in Darfur lies in 'awareness'. There are still too many people in the world who are unaware of the situation that is going on in Darfur. People need to educate themselves and become enlightened on the issues that people in Darfur are facing.

Once the whole world is aware of the injustices that are a part of life for Darfurians, then the world can stand against the Darfurian government, and raise a standard to stop the lawlessness that is prevalent there. The key is merely to spread the word and continue to provide support for all the helpless people in Darfur, who don't have their own voice, and need the rest of the world to speak up for them.

So, to all those who wonder why the situation in Darfur is of worldwide concern, the answer still remains: " How can it not be?"

Khono Mtetwa

Right Words: Darfur

They came on camels and in trucks with guns, they came with their weapons of war, they came with an air of brutality, they came with death clasped closely to their hearts. The cut of their engines sliced through the peaceful air and my naïve eyes watched them swarm my village, filling each hut with terror, pressing upon us their demonization. Screams and sobs fill my ears, it is inescapable, inevitable. In just a few moments my short life will have ended with the smell of fear and the vision of evil. But not yet. Life does not grant such luck. First, my wide-eyed innocence must witness malice that the Devil himself could not conceive.

I watched in the blackness, as I cannot tear my eyes away, but the darkness is surrounding, suffocating, threatening to consume me. I wish for it. I pray for it. I am numb, numb to the point where the scorched earth beneath my feet does not warm my cold and abandoned heart. They killed my mother quickly. BANG! And she left this blackened earth. She hit the ground with a thud and their laughter filled my ears. A haunting sound. They did not indulge in her and for that I am grateful. But I sat there, in the darkened room in which my now dead mother hid me when we saw their approach. I am paralysed, my legs not listening to the brain for me to protect the innocence of this world, little did I know that I was part of that lingering innocence. I sat there in my moment of private darkness and was made to bear witness to the things they did to my younger sister, to other girls and women. Bad things. Things that men should not do to little girls. Bleeding, screaming, bleeding, and screaming. "Bora Bora" they jeered.

It felt like hours that I sat there and watched, waited for them to stop. They kept some of the women alive. Punishing them further with a tainted life. My sister was one of the lucky ones. They slit her throat. She lay there defeated, naked and beaten.

Silence came like a rush. A relief from all the pain that would forever haunt me, both in this life and the next. It was then that my cowardly legs decided to obey my reluctant brain. The sun shone relentlessly but conquered as if the land itself had seen too many darkened days to possess the strength to continue. It dazzled my eyes as they tried to adjust to the blinding light. It was then that I saw them all. The silence now my own private hell. I wished for the screaming to return, something to show some sign of life. Their bodies lay mutilated, these were the people whom I was still growing up with, people whom I had grown to like and could have one day loved. Now their blood ran red, like a river through a desert. I looked around once more and contemplated all their untold stories and an overwhelming anger filled my weak heart.

It was then that my knees buckled and I fell to the ground, fell at my sister's body. Her eyes were glazed over, staring off to some distant paradise for which I had been refused entry. A small smile pulled at her lips as if she had seen the light before it was ready to take her. It was then that I felt it, the cold metal against the back of my head and I knew what was coming. I welcomed it. And in that moment, I looked up into my murderer's eyes and saw him admiring his work with a gleam of satisfaction and a job well done. And in that second I realized that life is not worth living if you don't have freedom, that death come to us al—

Candice McKechnie

'We are all responsible
to everyone for everything'

As Fyodor Dostoevsky once wrote "We are all responsible to everyone for everything." So why are the terrible, inhuman circumstances in Darfur unknown to so many people worldwide? Statistics are recorded in their millions, with 2.4 being displaced and 4.4 in desperate need of relief. Yet because we are not affected directly, you and I will not think twice about the reports, and leave the suffering and tragedy between the sheets of this newspaper.

Imagine your alarm this morning the hateful, barbaric voice of a government soldier, violently beating you for the sheer joy of it. Imagine waking to find your whole sense of security and comfort – gone. Imagine the dread of not knowing if it is safe to step outside your own home. While the world sleeps peacefully, dreaming of other places, children not unlike yours are being rounded up to be taken to militia groups.

Ignorance is bliss.

Men, women and children all suffer awfully, regardless of their vulnerability. The displacement camps are flooded with hundreds of orphans who have witnessed their own parents savagely murdered by the Janjaweed. These children will now live a life without a family, will grow older with the absent love of a fond parent. When in fear, a child will undoubtedly look to their parents. Who will they turn to now? The cold-heart of a guard who beats them on a daily basis?

Every one of us has a mother. Think of her, how ruined you'd feel to discover that she's been gang-raped by a group of malicious, dirty men? Rape has now become a weapon of war ladies and gentlemen, and its consequences are terrible. Infants that are results of rape are slaughtered without care, after all, it is their fault of course. A comment reads on an Amnesty International campaign leaflet; "If she goes to collect water she will be raped. If she doesn't her children will die." A wretched situation for a mother to be in – who can put a price on a child's life? Anyone's life?

Unable to protect or defend their families, men are butchered. If strong enough they are taken and forced to work for the militia group that has been lucky enough to find them. If not, the shadow that jeers at them, lying powerless in the dust, will be the last face they ever see.

Drowned in what has been called a 'blood bath', communities have been torn to shreds, all signs of human consciousness have vanished. There is no mercy in their life, no sparing or second chances.

After decades of poverty, drought and small scale conflicts, the situation in Darfur began about 5 years ago, in February 2003, when the Sudanese Government began a campaign of 'ethnic cleansing'. Many put the conflict in Darfur down to the unsettled differences between 'Arab' and 'Non-Arab' African people, but this is not the case. Two rebel groups: The Sudanese Liberation Army (SLA) and the Justice and Equality Movement (JEM) finally made a point of argument against the central government. The JEM and SLA could ultimately represent the farmers, who are mostly 'Non-Arab' Muslims. Attacking with brutal force, the government proves a powerfully vicious enemy. To ensure they could defeat the rebel groups, the President, Al-Bashir, made orders to increase weapons and support for the local tribes and militias, widely known as the Janjaweed, who are mostly 'Arab' Muslims. The notorious members of the Janjaweed, have systematically tortured, murdered and raped thousands of Darfuris, wiping out entire villages and destroying many food and water supplies. Tactics of the government include painting various aircraft white copying the UN logo to the underneath. Approaching villages, the Darfuris expect relief and rush to the plane only to be bombed in their hundreds.

2.3 million Darfuris have fled their villages, many spilling over to the neighbouring country of Chad. Many now live in displaced person camps, (IDP's), relying on the UN and Humanitarian Organizations for shelter, food, water and safety. Yet still they cannot be guaranteed full safety, with savage attacks still occurring in many IDP's. Another 1 million Darfuris still live in fear of their lives in their villages, with only a poorly funded African Union peacekeeping group (AMIS). With only 7,400 troops, and a lack of money to provide arms, many ask the whereabouts of the police force. The answer: when present, it is useless. Ignoring calls of emergency and refusing to follow up reports of murder and rape, thousands of cases remain unsolved and crime statistics are soaring.

Despite the grave circumstances in Darfur, a lot can be done to assist and bring the country through the hellish ordeal they face. Groups such as Amnesty International, Human Rights Watch and other NGOs are furiously campaigning and influencing as many citizens as possible. The awareness of the affairs in Darfur has grown widely, media attention growing and putting pressure on the Sudanese government. The Human Rights Watch has produced a report of 'peacekeeping challenges' that informs everyone involved of the 'benchmarks' that are being put in place. It's all very well in ink on a piece of paper, but will these actions work? What is to say that people will not follow through in their promises? It looks to me as though the individuals who have the power to politically make a stand are not applying it to something worthwhile. When will someone realize that it is NOW that something has to be done? "It's not convenient" some say. Yes, you are right. It's incredibly inconvenient that a mother of four has to wonder if she will ever see her children again every time she steps out her door. It's inconvenient that millions of people's lives have changed forever, not knowing it was ever going to happen. Suitability isn't an issue here, it's acting upon a true human instinct that something is extremely wrong.

The future is in our hands, and I ask you, please get involved to help. We can increase the pressure upon the Government in Darfur to withdraw their support from any groups and to create a plan that will enable the circumstances to return to normal – safe. It's the least any human being deserves, it's what we expect. We were all given the capability to make a difference. Use it.

Megan Holland

Another Sunrise, Another Death

Another sunrise means another death. Another sunrise means another rape. Another sunset rests with lootings, beatings and not forgetting our mothers' cries. Why can't anyone hear them? The cries are loud enough and I hear them at the back of my head every night when I sleep. We have become prisoners in the place we call home. We are prisoners in our land. The cry for freedom cannot be heard by those that take pleasure in taking lives but it can only be heard by people like me, those that have seen it all.

Two years ago the Human Rights Watch Researchers came to school and asked us to draw what our homes looked like. Unlike some children, my parents had been killed in a bombing near our tents. I didn't draw the families that the other children drew. I have no one. All I have is myself. I drew a picture of what my life was about; armed men on horses and camels attacking our villages. Mothers and children on their backs fleeing helicopters and falling bombs: the bombs orphaned me. A woman crying and standing defenceless after a Janjaweed officer has just raped her and possibly given her a disease. Diseases that cannot be treated might be her only way to peace and rest; death. The police will do nothing about it. They tell her to look for the man and to bring him to them. It is impossible for her because many have taken advantage of her and the memories of their faces haunt her. What used to be her bravery and courage is crippled by the trauma. Why can't anyone hear her cries?

Another minute could be my last minute. Another second could be my last breath. There comes a time when they shoot at everything that moves, everything that has breath. They steal our crops and livestock. What's left for me? If they take everything I have, they might as well take me too, for I am certain that it will give me peace. I will not have to cry anymore. I will not have to hear the sounds of the gunshots and the sounds of the howling helicopters that fly above me. I will no longer be given false hopes that the UN are coming to save me. Coming to bring back what used to be my life. For what I am living now is not life. I am awake but my world is dead. It is better for me to join my world and only then can I be at peace with myself.

They say that they come to 'cleanse' but all I have seen them do is kill. No one is safe. But what keeps me alive are my two feet – the feet that have never felt the comfort of a shoe for three years; the feet that have walked on the land that is filled with the bones and the blood of people like me. The land has been destroyed and savaged. This land has caused many deaths. The earth itself is scattered and it is the reason for our cries. Why can't anyone hear them?

The AMIS says they have come to save us and to protect us but we all know that they are not an effective protection force. Rape and sexual violence against women and girls has been a prominent feature of their 'ethnic cleansing.' What has the AMIS done to protect me from this? They have done nothing. All the protection I have is myself. The shields I have are my two feet that run when I see the Janjaweed coming. God is my only witness.

The only thing that comforts me is the sound of the women singing. Despite their fear and insecurities of living in the camps, they still rejoice. They draw pictures of their crops and flowers and the land that used to be beautiful. Only the memory of these can comfort them. The only joy they have is the joy of being around each others' company. Many of these women and their daughters have been demeaned and would be lucky to run away from the Janjaweed when they start their attacks. They beat them calling them slaves and rebels that deserve beatings. They have burned their houses in front of them. I will never forget the bad images of the burning houses and fleeing at night because our village was burned. I am lucky enough not to have experienced any beatings so far but this still doesn't guarantee my safety. I don't think that any human being deserves such injustice and inhumanity. Why do such joyful and harmless people deserve this torture? Why can't people hear what lies behind our cries?

White aircraft flying above me used to bring such relief because usually the UN people would come out and sometimes they would give us food. People ran to the aircraft because they were happy that these people had come to save them and give them food and water. I stood at the back of our tent because I knew that the people I lived with had gone to get the food and would then share it among ourselves. They all gathered around the helicopter waiting for the officers to come out. Ten men dressed in military uniforms came out holding guns and whips. They began to beat people like dogs. They made gunshots in the air to scare them. Some managed to escape while others were on the ground embracing the last seconds of their lives. I heard the cries and could not imagine how any human being could want another to feel such pain and hurt. They came towards our camps looking for more people to attack. I was very terrified and began to run and managed to escape without letting them touch me.

We cannot trust anyone now because we do not know who has come to save us or kill us. Anyone could come and kill us any time and place. Our lives lie in our own hands.

I am living in this world alone. They have taken all I have: my parents, my happiness, the comfort of feeling at home and my security. Everyone has a right to all of this except for us. The reason for the beating – we are of different ethnicity. This is beyond our power and yet we are suffering because of this. We have suffered enough, why can't anyone hear us?

Sandra Mayenda

Life

Ubuntu

She turned a blind eye to the homeless man begging on the street corner. She has complete vision in both eyes; she can see from all angles, yet she passed the filthy, dishevelled man and failed to even glance in his direction. He implored her to spare any coins she had, but she didn't even offer him the courtesy and respect of replying. Perhaps she is deaf, as well as blind.

Isn't it ironic how close we all are to becoming homeless? Bad luck, ill fortune, hasty investments. These can all create a rift in our finances, leading to bankruptcy and imminent destitution. Take a good look at that nameless, grubby man who sits on the street corner day after day, his cardboard box and aging newspapers the only security he has at his disposal. His black eyes are empty and see nothing, as life steadfastly passes him by. His heart is bleeding, mourning, crying out for someone to look at him, notice him, help him.

My fascination for the down-and-out stems from my own childhood and the realisation that when your life begins to deteriorate and fall apart, one really can hear the shattering of their glass house. When a child has everything that currency can buy, then loses everything by faults not their own, the appreciation of all things- big and small- ensues. When one experiences trying times, this is also the most opportune of times to discover true alliances and the most compassionate of people.

This brings me to a belief system prevalent in South Africa called 'Ubuntu', which centres on the proverb, "Umuntu ungumuntu ngabanye abantu," meaning that an individual can only be classified as a human being by their actions and mannerisms, and the way in which they interact with others, namely people in times of hardship or need. 'Ubuntu' encourages one to search deep within themselves and excavate all the good and kindness that it is believed even the most callous of people possess. 'Ubuntu' is an idealism that is practised throughout Africa, and which has even spread to other parts of the world — displaying the interest people have in doing good.

How many times have you ever passed a homeless man or someone in need of help and averted your gaze? Most just carry on stepping and return to their seemingly perfect lives, where they forget all about the troubles of others to focus on their own greatness. People think that the only way to assist a person in need is with money. Some people feel that if there isn't a jingle in their pocket, they cannot make an impact in anyone's life. This could not be further from the truth. In fact, this is quite contrary, because when a person has no earthly treasures or securities to hide behind, they are in their most natural form and can be themselves without any pretence.

I was hanging out with my friends after an arduous day of shopping, and as I glanced beside me, I noticed a homeless man sitting by a bin, a half-eaten hamburger, that I assume he had retrieved from the bin, clutched firmly in his hand. I walked over to him and placed some money into his donation hat, and as I did so, I looked into his eyes and saw a troubled soul, an individual who was once admired and respected by those who knew him, but was now a mere shell of his former self. My sympathy was aroused, as I detected the shame he felt at having to accept charity from a schoolgirl. As he reluctantly looked up at me, our eyes met. It was when I smiled at him that his facial expression altered and it was a different man who smiled back at me. The look of desolation left his eyes, and there was a new warmth about him. His rough, sun-beaten, weathered face somehow didn't appear to be so wrinkled and filthy anymore, and his teeth were of a pearly white. "Thank you," he said, and he meant it. It was then that I realized that with the cash I'd given him, he could probably afford a hot meal and something to drink, but my smile was priceless to him, as it made him feel human again to have someone notice him as a human being, instead of pitying him as a failure down on his luck.

'Ubuntu' teaches that everyone – no matter how old or young – can make a difference. One doesn't have to live a picture-perfect existence in order to make an impact in someone else's life. All a person needs in order to alter the way a person thinks or feels, is to care. In life, people don't care enough. Some children are reduced to living and begging on the streets, because their parents and relatives don't care enough.

Young girls are drinking and smoking underage, while out partying each night, because they don't care about and respect themselves enough to treat themselves with the proper care and dignity.

Presidents and government officials are disputing and at war over land and natural resources, while innocent civilians lose limbs and loved ones.

If that one distant relative took that child in, or their 'druggie' mother and father got help to overcome their addictions, and got a job to support their offspring, that innocent child wouldn't have to call a street corner 'home'.

If that young girl took a look in the mirror and realized that she is special and that she should respect herself, and got the proper supervision and affection from her parents, then she wouldn't be throwing her life away for the sake of a good time.

If the rest of the world intervened when countries are at war, then the carnage and annihilation of people's lives would not take place.

> One way.
> One chance.
> One act.
> One person.
> This is all it takes to make a change in the world.
> "Umuntu ungumuntu ngabanye abantu."

Khono Mtetwa

This piece was a winner in the Portsmouth City Council Writing Competition, 2008.

Maria Virginia Alfonzo Reina

I used to be a dreamer.

Part One

***

One

My parents split up when I was very young.

I won't pretend to remember it well. To me, everything seemed to be going along fine. I recall moving, with my father and my mother, into some little flat that used to be a dentistry department. It wasn't a particularly big place, but that didn't matter to me. There was only one time that I realized that something was wrong (not that I ever imagined that they would split up, being only around four years old), and that was when I walked into my parents' bedroom and my mother was curled up at the foot of the bed, crying.

That was the very first time I ever saw my mother cry. It astounded me, because she'd always seemed so strong. *I* was the baby, *I* was the one that cried.

My dad was in the poky little kitchen, looking angry, clutching the edge of the Formica counter. The tension was thick in the air, and I didn't understand what was going on.

I cannot remember when they were officially divorced , and neither can I recall being told why, though I expect I was. Since then, I have formed my own reasons for the break-up.

You see, they married young. My mother was pregnant with me at eighteen. I saw a wedding photograph once, and she was pregnant then,

24

in her white dress. So, I suppose that I must've been a mistake, and that they only married because they didn't want the shame of a child born out of wedlock.

Of course, their's was only a young romance, and it could never have lasted forever – and I would know all about young romances, now, too.

They made their mistakes, and I am the living proof of that.

*

Two

After that, we went to live with my grandmother. I didn't like not being able to always see my father much. I was his little princess, and he was like my best friend.

My mother was there for me more often, I suppose, but whenever I got to see my father, we had *adventures*. He used to take me to his grandfather's farm. Primarily it was a mango farm, but there was a herd of cows, a chicken coop, fish tanks and thirty-seven horses. There were guard dogs, too, and they patrolled the farm at night to keep out intruders. They frightened me a lot: back at my grandmother's house I'd always had dogs, but these dogs liked to *bite*.

But they also fascinated me – it was strange. I was scared, but I thought that they were so like wolves. During the day I'd sometimes stand by their cage and watch them, but I was always warned not to get too close: they didn't know my scent, I was just an intruder to them.

The horses also fascinated me. I'd always been a dreamer, and I loved the white horses the best, because I thought they were really unicorns in disguise, or that they were winged horses and that if I asked them nicely enough they could show me their wings and fly me away.

I also believed that I could charm them.

I thought this because once, I rode with my father as we took the cattle to a field. My father kidded that he was no horseman, and let me take the reins: I tugged a bit and whispered to the horse to be nice: to my surprise, the mare trotted on like I'd asked, and I was so thrilled.

Once, my father took me riding to the fields, and we saw the long, jagged skeleton of a snake, stretched out in the parched grass. I was scared that the mare would take fright, but my father just whispered, "So... so...", which is a word that really *does* charm horses, and the mare just trotted past.

I was proud to be my father's daughter, even if my mother said that he never tried hard enough. To me, he was like the hero in every story.

I always thought that my dad was really, really *cool*, for lack of a better word. He was also kind of reckless, and I loved it. Back in the city, he let me use his rifle to shoot at trees from the top floor of his parent's house, and I made the pines across the street shake and shiver by hitting them with the little metal bead-like bullets.

He smoked, which is something that I now find extremely vulgar. But when I was little I didn't really mind: I loved it when my father leaned back on his chair and breathed out little circles of smoke for my amusement. Sometimes, he even used a pipe.

A few times, he took me up the beautiful mountain that is near my grandmother's house, the *Avila*, and we'd walk all the way up it. I was really small and chubby, and I struggled to keep up, and I hated it that he had to keep stopping for me because I wanted to be brave and strong even though I tripped over a rock and cut my knee. But it didn't matter, not when we got to the top and stood above the clouds.

My father and I didn't always go out on adventures. Sometimes, we stayed in and played video games till I was too tired for another round of *Bloody Roar* or *Tomb Raider*, and then he'd take me to the hammock and rock me to sleep whilst he decidedly worked on some graphic design on his computer.

My father was really like me in so many ways. He figured that it was because we were both Sagittarians (since I'd been born on November 26th and he in early December), and we both had the fiery spirit of the horse-archer in us. I think this notion made us both very happy.

I was his little princess. I miss him, really, even though I often tell myself I hate him. It is so strange to me that he has forgotten everything. I always wonder if he thinks about me from time to time... but I know that he doesn't. He is so busy with his new little princess to remember.

It kills me that my father... my <u>hero</u>... failed me, too.

*

Three

I was only with my father every few weeks. The rest of the time, I lived in the capital of Venezuela, a city called Caracas. It is the only city that feels truly like home, even if it is dangerous and its outskirts are surrounded by *barrios*, what the Venezuelans call the slums. I've only returned to my home country once, when I was thirteen, and it was strange to be back: things had changed, but yet some things were so familiar. I lived in Venezuela until I was eight years of age. My home there was the house of my grandmother, my Abuelita Yaya, as I called her. It is the place where I grew up and learnt many things, and every single room holds so many memories for me.

I come from a large family, though in England I live only with my sisters, my mother and my stepfather. I have many uncles, aunts and cousins, all of whom I used to see often. There was my Tia Christina, who used to always help me make cookies and let me lick out the succulent mixture from the bowl, and my grandfather, Abuelito Antonio, who secretly fed me chocolate and sweets, because he had diabetes and couldn't eat them himself. I think it pleased him, to feed me treats, and to be completely frank, it pleased me too. And every night, before I was ushered to bed late by my mother, I would give him a kiss goodnight and then draw the sign of the cross on his forehead so that God would protect his dreams. Abuelito would always do it back to me all wrong, every single night, just to annoy me, but nevertheless I liked our strange ritual. There was also my Tia Susana, Tia Ana, la Tata, Pali... They used to treat me like a princess, all the time.

There is no doubt about it, I must have been the happiest girl in the entire world, even despite the divorce of my parents. I cannot remember any constant sadness in my life back then, save one: the day when my cousin, Juan Manuel, or *Juanchi*, as we called him, died.

27

I'll have to write this quickly, without interruption, without hesitation, in case I cry.

I must have been about seven years old. I was at my grandmother's house, and suddenly, everything was quiet. My grandmother was crying freely, as was my grandfather. I knew something was terribly, terribly wrong. But everybody was hushed, hardly speaking... and then only saying, "How can we tell Elena?" They were referring to my aunt, the grandmother of my cousins Juanchi and Diego. I don't know what I was doing at the time, but a while later, my godmother Mima ushered me into the kitchen. It was strange, because Mima had always seemed so cheerful, always tickling me and saying "*Tiki, tiki, tiki*," and wiggling her fingers at me. Only, she wasn't smiling any more. And there was my grandfather, in the kitchen. My grandmother was sat weeping fiercely at a chair by his side.

"*Juanchi se murió,*" my grandfather said.

Juanchi is dead.

Juanchi is DEAD.

I went to the funeral. My other cousins, Kiri and Carlos, didn't go. I was the only young one there, save Diego, Juanchi's brother. I sat next to him, and it struck me as strange that he was so motionless. Diego just sat there, staring, staring at the floor, hardly blinking. I tried speaking to him, and he did offer me a few words. But it was like he was trying to deliberately not talk about the death. Maybe he thought that if he didn't *say* it, then it wouldn't be *true* that Juanchi was dead.

I wasn't so sure of what had happened. A car accident, I knew that. I heard the adults talking... Juanchi had been asleep, against the car door, when a car collided directly against his skull.

I wonder if he knew what happened.

Maybe it didn't even hurt. Maybe he died instantly.

Maybe.

Tia Elena said something that I remember so strongly. She said that Juanchi hadn't wanted to go, that he'd wanted to stay a few more days with her in her apartment. She said she should have begged that he stayed.

And then, he wouldn't have died.

I thought about this for a long time. But somebody said that God had decided that if it was time for him to die, he would have done. Anything could have happened. He could have slipped in the shower. Anything.

I hated this so called *God* then, just for a second.

I remember that I had a flower. A red chrysanthemum, that somebody there had given me.

The coffin was in the middle of a plain white room, with people on all sides, crying hard. I saw the coffin there, gleaming beneath the glare of the light, and I went to it. The lid was open, and I peered inside. There was Juanchi, lying inside, smartly dressed, eyes closed. I thought it would look like he was asleep. But it didn't. His face was horribly pale, and his lips looked puffy and purplish-blue. And then there was the scar; on his forehead, roughly sealed up with what looked to me like thick string. It ran from his head to his eyebrows, and it was hideous: a dash of raw colour against the cold shades of Juanchi's skin.

I started to cry really hard then. Because the person lying in the stupid long box wasn't Juanchi. That person there, cold and colourless, couldn't be my very same thirteen-year-old cousin that had insisted that I practise actually hitting the ball in baseball, nor the cousin that I shouted at for reading my diary, nor the cousin that thought he was great on a skateboard.

That person there, that dead child, couldn't be the cousin that hugged me and made me feel so safe in his arms as I slept during those hot afternoons in Puerto La Cruz while we watched television.

As grown-ups tore me away from the coffin, I lay my red chrysanthemum on the glass that separated me from the body.

 I don't remember much of what happened after the funeral. I know that we caught a plane back to Caracas from Puerto La Cruz. I can't say anything really comes to mind afterwards, not even tears, save one thing. A dream.

And my dream was so, so vivid… not a dream, but a *vision*.

I swear.

Often, my grandmother would hold parties at our house. It was a big place, and it was always the heart of the family. Everyone would always come, everyone, for birthdays, and Christmases, and New Year's parties…

The room was full, crowded, and I was walking towards the doors that lead to the patio from the main hall. And then the edges blurred, and there was Juanchi. I cannot remember it in as vivid detail as I know I saw it. But he was there, right before me, and I didn't know it was a dream. I started to speak, but he stopped me, looking at me and lifting his fingers slowly towards his mouth.

He pursed his lips, and hissed,

"*Shh…*"

And then he wasn't there anymore. The edges of my dream stopped being so faded and white, and became clear. And there was Diego there, speaking to me.

But even in my dream, I was thinking,

"He came to tell me goodbye. He came to tell me *goodbye*."

And that was the last time I ever saw my cousin Juanchi. It could have been just a dream, I know that is what people think. A dream, a coincidence. But it wasn't. Maybe it sounds like I'm just being stupid, but I don't care. I know that he came to tell me goodbye.

*

Four

Life in Venezuela was fun.

It really was as simple as that.

Every day, I found new adventures, new games… new obsessions. Like when I first discovered Japanese Anime; it was all I ever thought about. I'd rush home at midday, when school ends in Venezuela, and after lunch I'd settle down and watch my daily doses of *Sailor Moon, Dragonball Z, Rurouni Kenshin* (which back there was called *Samurai X*, which is actually the name of the film and not the series) and *Pokémon*. Afterwards I'd settle on Abuelita Yaya's big bed, with the air conditioning on, and we'd drink a glass of Nesquik and eat some Oreos whilst watching *Johnny Bravo* or *The Magic School Bus.* Abuelita always pretended to have a crush on Johnny Bravo, because he had hair just like Elvis Presley, and I found this hilarious but believable, seeing as I always said I was in love with Trunks and Goku from *Dragonball Z.*

My grandmother loved drawing and painting, and we used to always draw together. Sometimes she would ask me to sit still and pose for her, which was a feat that I found impossible. Once, she made a strange... well, painting, I suppose. It was, principally, plaster of Paris which had been flattened onto a piece of card and then shaped, to make some strange sort of lumpy composition. Abuelita painted the background a rich purple, and at the base of the piece there was a strange ellipse-shape, which she painted green and then she made streaks of red and yellow come out of it, like particularly colourful beams of light at a show in a stadium.

It was extremely weird, very abstract, and maybe a tad tasteless as a piece to hang on the wall, but I really loved it, because *she'd* made it.

Painting wasn't the only thing that my grandmother was good at. She was good at dress-making and sewing, and she had a sewing machine in the spare room which used to really frighten me, and as well as that, she was an excellent chef. I'm not kidding, even her simplest recipes are fit for royalty. Which is really fitting, since our family name is *Reina*, the Spanish word for queen.

I could go on for hours about how excellent Abuelita's cooking is. She used to make this cake called *Marquesa*, which was layers of melted dark chocolate and cooked condensed milk over digestive biscuits. It sounds a little strange, but it is undoubtedly the best thing that you will ever taste.It didn't even stop there. Her banana cake was always the best, and it wasn't just sweet foods that she had a knack for making – it was everything. She used to cook hen, which to me looked exactly like chicken until she showed me the insides of the raw bird, in which you could just make out tiny, tiny would-be eggs. And she would make *Mondongo*, which was a delicious, thick stew with a name that I've always thought sounds amusing but unappetizing.

Traditional Venezuelan food was the best, though. *Cachapas, enpanadas* and *arepa* ...

Names that people here in England will find pretty hard to pronounce, but very easy to eat. Cachapas look a lot like pancakes, but made with cornflower and not intended to be sweet. Enpanadas are fried cornflower dough rolls filled with something – *anything* – you like. My favourite filling was always mince meat, but you really can have anything savoury, which is why they are so delicious. I distinctly remember that my mother loved eating them with shark filling, but I never really liked that.

And then there were arepas, which were probably cooked most often since they are so simple to make. They're just a ball of the special cornflower dough fried on the pan in olive oil. I have to admit that Abuelita Yaya really did make the very best, even if I always complained that the arepas were too hot and scraped out the insides and ate that with butter.

My life was a good one.

I really did have all the things I wanted.

Until my mother met *him*. An Englishman. Tall, not old, but with little hair.

When my mother introduced me to him, I couldn't even pronounce his name, so that wasn't a particularly great start.

A lot of things in life are unfair, and I know this. A lot of people are much worse off, too. But knowing these facts don't make letting go of things any easier. After all, how can you deal with letting go of the things that you know, and the reasons that you smile?

But sometimes people make choices for you, and you have to tear yourself away. Even if you never smile that much again.

*

Five

I *didn't* like England.

Christmas in England seemed extremely boring to me – I was so used to the annual parties that my grandmother held, in which all the children in the family stayed up just as long as all the adults, and at the stroke of

32

midnight we would all run up the stairs to the bedrooms and find the gifts that Baby Jesus had left on our beds. I didn't like the way that Santa Claus operated. I didn't want to go to bed so early – knowing that there would be presents under a pine tree in the morning was like caffeine.

I also didn't understand the point of Christmas Dinner – I hardly ate any of it, because the Yorkshire puddings were soggy, the turkey was bland, and the stuffing looked plain gross.

I couldn't help comparing the customs of Venezuela to those of frosty, cold, grey England.

New Year's celebrations didn't impress me, either. It might have been the Millennium, but it was pretty dull for me. After watching fireworks and the Millennium Dome on television for what must have been hours, we went to a party with people we didn't know. At least, it was boring for the children, who were allocated to a separate room and sat down to go on the PlayStation. I just sat there by myself because the other kids wouldn't let me play Ray-Man.

It's really strange to look back and believe I ever cried about something as stupid as wanting to be with my mother. Especially because, as time changed, we grew apart, and sometimes my mother became the thing I wanted to be furthest from.

*

Six

My mother married in Venezuela about three or four months after we returned from England. It wasn't a church wedding, and my mother didn't wear white – instead, she was clad in a long, narrow silk dress, a pale, pale green in colour.

She looked beautiful and delicate as she descended the stairs.

The wedding itself was held at my grandmother's house, and immediately beforehand there was a photo shoot: my mother, ever photogenic, draped herself over Abuelita Yaya's marble floors and looked every bit like a model from *Vogue*.

Malcolm didn't look nearly as impressive – he was in a black suit, but coincidentally had a tie that matched my mother's dress hue exactly.

Everybody was thrilled apart from me, because their marriage could mean only one thing for me.

I really *was* moving to England.

Goodbyes are not an easy thing.

Goodbyes are… unreal. They have much in similarity with death. Because when you tell someone goodbye, you might never see them again. Maybe goodbyes are *worse* than death – the dead may be gone, but not forgotten. But… the people that you say goodbye to might never think about you again for the rest of their lives. Someone you loved beyond being able to explain it may move on and forget your eyes, your smile, your voice, your name… your very existence.

I had to say goodbye to a lot of people. And it was my father – my best friend, my hero against all odds – that forgot all about his little girl.

He went with me to the airport. None of the memories of this are vivid- maybe I was too blinded by tears to take in detail.

Abuelita Yaya was taking me away, almost dragging me through check-in, as I screamed, and screamed, and screamed relentlessly, thrashing and twisting to look back.

And there he was. My father.

My father. Mi padre. Standing, staring after me. Was he crying? I don't know.

I never saw him again.

End of Part One

Part Two

Seven

Now, moving to England was not entirely bad.

We moved to Portsmouth, a city to the south, by the grey sea. My first home in England was a flat, the top floor unless you count the penthouse. It overlooked the sea, the pier, and the Canoe Lake – a long and shallow stretch of water with little boats and swans.

I didn't really like it there at first; the place was fine, but I only had Malcolm and my mother now, as opposed to my large family in Venezuela. Most of the time I felt bored, and almost like an intruder.

Again, I was just my mother's luggage. But that was alright at first, because it meant that sometimes we actually spent time together. In Venezuela, my mother had always tried to involve me in girly things such as trips out shopping. Things I hadn't really enjoyed back then. But now, to try and help me to learn English, my mother used to buy me books and we'd climb onto my bed and she would read aloud to me. I hardly understood, and when it was my turn to read I'd mess it all up, but it didn't matter. I just loved it that my beautiful mother would take time to be with me. It was at those moments that I really did feel *loved*.

For a while, my father kept in contact. He called, and even though it wasn't as often as I would've liked, it had to be enough.

"Guess what?" He said once.

"Tell me, papa!" I ordered.

"You may not be here, but when you come visit, I will give you thirty-seven horses!" He exclaimed. "From the farm. They're all yours."

It was a strange gift, but I was delighted. Any present from my father was most special to me. It showed me he really did miss me. Only, soon after that, his calls became less and less frequent.

But he still called... on rare occasions.

I was still his princess, wasn't I?

School was... strange, to begin with. On my first day at St. Swithun's, my new Year Four classmates all stared at me like I was some kind of new toy. At play time they crowded me and shouted their names at me – they all sounded and looked more or less the same to me, so remembering them was difficult.

The first friend I ever made in England was Rosie: tall, pale, freckly, bespectacled and with wavy brown hair pulled back into a ponytail.

The word 'what' was probably the most familiar to me thus far: since I hardly understood what people said, and I was always curious to discover that names of things, it was a word that came in handy.

After the crowd of inquisitive children dispersed, Rosie was the first to approach me. It was probably because I wore yellow Pikachu hair-clips and they called to her like a magnet or something. She began talking, and it is safe to say that I didn't understand a single word. And so, undoubtedly, I said,

"What?"

She repeated herself, as did I. After several attempts to get through to me, she cracked, and held me by the shoulders. She leaned in.

"What's your problem?" She said.

I blinked stupidly at her, but then she grinned. "What is *your* problem?" I repeated. And then we laughed – heaps of giggles, the only thing really understood in any language.

So that was the somewhat weird beginning of mine and Rosie's strong friendship. I made the second friend on the morning immediately after.

My mother used to walk me to school, and every morning without fail, a cute, freckled girl with curly brown hair would stand by the gate and wait for me. Her name was Millie, and along with Rosie, they helped me make friends. I couldn't speak that well, nor write, but it was okay, because I wasn't lonely. Rosie was clever, and always scored highest in the Spelling Tests when I did poorly, and Millie was confident and popular – things I would've been, had I been capable to pronounce all the names of my peers. So I worked really hard and read a lot so that I'd improve my language skills, and even though after a while my mother stopped reading alongside me, it paid off. I made lots of friends, and I took part in many crazy and creative games.

Rosie and I became intrepid students at *Hogwart's School For Witchcraft And Wizardry* – we were both captivated by *Harry Potter* and worked hard to come up with games that J.K. Rowling would have been proud of. Millie, I soon discovered, liked Japanese Anime too, so we spent two entire years playing *Cardcaptors* during playtime – I was Sakura, and I pretended to have a pink staff that could seal magic spirits onto cards, and Millie was Tomoyo, my best friend and battle-costume designer. With Lilly I was a secret detective, with Hannah a mass producer of delicious candy, and with Henry I was Superkitten, a cat superhero out to save the world from starvation.

There was one game that we designed, however, that brought all of my friends together.

It was a game in which we were Gods and Goddesses by design. It seems stupid now, but I think that at the time, we became so wrapped up in the game that It seemed like real life.

I was deeply immersed in my role – I was Virgi (a modified version of my second name), a powerful goddess. I owned a magic phoenix named Mulana, and my realm was named Corus. With Henry's help, I even forged a map, two metres in each direction, showing in detail places such as the Temple of Time, the Fountain of Life, and the Valley of Rainbows. It seems so strange that I could create these things up until I was eleven. A place so real to me it was better than home. Better than all those places in books I read, better than *Narnia*. Now, I wish I could go back there so badly. Just close my eyes, and be back there in the golden fields I used to imagine, with serpentine dragons soaring overhead, roaring their war-chant,

"Dire, dire,

Heart on fire,

Bring to me

My hearts desire."

Creating that chant with Millie, my proclaimed *Fire-Sister*, is such a vivid memory.

My heart's desire? It was to escape there, and not be wrapped in misery anymore.

Isabella was born in September as I started Year Six. I remember the conversation I had with my mother nine months prior, in the small dining room of our second house. It was exactly as follows.

"You know that thing you've always wanted?" My mother asked me.

I was excited.

"You've bought me an X-Box!" I said dumbly, though in perfect English.

My language skills had soared, and people found it hard to believe that before I'd hardly been able to ask the time a few years previously.

"*No.* You're going to have a little brother or sister."

This was, needless to say, a shock, and it took a while to register. I think that when I was very young and my mother had still been with my father, I really had wanted a younger sibling. But after eleven entire years of being the youngest in the family, it was strange to know there was a baby on the way.

I read all the books on baby-care that my mother purchased, ready to take big-sisterhood in my stride. I imagined myself older, in my twenties, looking after my younger sibling, and I was pleased with what I saw. But it was different when I got to St. Mary's Hospital and joined my mother in the ward to find Isabella, who was beautiful in a strange, tiny, pinkish way.

I used to always dream of... a happy ending. It's what every little princess wants, is it not? Well... it doesn't matter. I'm not my father's little princess any more.

I used to be alone. I wanted to be just like everyone else. I wasn't happy being me, I didn't believe that anyone would really want me for what I am. But I won't follow, I won't conform with others in order to seem a nonconformist.

I'm not a mistake. I'm not a burden, If I lose myself in what I write, then there is a chance that one day I'll make my mother proud. And one day my father will remember me, and see how well I did without him.

Right now, all I want to do is hang out with my friends. I'm just a regular teenager. They're the reasons I need to smile.

And besides, who needs a happy ending at my age? I'm just fifteen, after all.

The Beginning.

Big School

In September 2002 I, Josh Bartholomew, was entered into St. Edmund's secondary school. From leaving Corpus Christi I was rather confident about the whole switchover from primary to 'Big' school. The feeling I had was that of immortality; what could be different about day-to-day life in a secondary school that I hadn't experienced in primary school...?

However, I could not have been more wrong in being so secure in my own head about the changeover. My stance at the time had a big impact on my attitude at the time. I was in Year 6, eleven years old, in the oldest year group in the school. I was answerable to no one except the teaching hierarchy. I was physically bigger than some of the six-year-olds there and even some of the eleven-year-olds. The teaching at primary school is not just teaching; I'd see it as a coffee morning with Mrs. Cox. We were taught by one teacher, a teacher that knew our mums, a teacher that taught on a very personal level. The teachers were kind, comical and sympathetic. Sooner rather than later, I was to receive the cold sharp shock that I had coming to me...

On a hazy morning, at the start of a lazy September week, I approached the gates. Being used to walking a maximum of ten minutes to the bright, colourful, artistic gates of primary school, I was deceived into thinking this would be the same. People had told me, it's no sweat it's not, moving to 'big school'. But as I looked up at the cold, uninviting industrial gates I knew that they were just sympathizers, in other words, liars.

As I walked through the gates, shirt neatly tucked in, tie done up accordingly laced with a neat, fresh blazer to match I looked around. I did this kind of, 'looking around' as I slowly, absent-mindedly walked through the primary school gates. But with each step I took deeper into the meat grinder that faced me, I realized that this place is going to make or break me. The enthusiasm I gathered during the summer holidays slowly, but surely, disintegrated before me eyes. What was left before me was the cold harsh reality that was to be, 'Big School'.

My mind was turning into a First World War trench; I had my thoughts on the front line, of a happy, gleeful secondary school life. But, I also had reserve thoughts behind the 'what ifs'. The reserve thoughts were slowly getting 'reinforcements' thanks to the 'wonderful, joyous surroundings'. What I was left with in the short space of 5 minutes was a big mixture of emotions, a blur of feeling and reaction. Distraught, the whole blueprint of another happy five years of my life burnt in front of me, its ashes turned green with envy and resentment.

As I breached the threshold, I was half expecting a greeting from the teachers, instead a crooked smile, etched across their tired dreary faces, almost cast in stone. I suddenly realized this was not just a place for mindless gossip, fun and innocent games. but this was the place where dreams come true, or man is broken.

In secondary school I met lots of people. This, however, was not a negative change; it did not rattle my walls, and I learnt to accept other people. I learnt to breach the narrow-minded walls of conformity. People were not only there to engage in idle conversation but marvels of time, and they were breaking out of their moulds, just as I was. I noticed people changing through the five years of being at secondary school. The school machine was a masterful, ungracious, lump of production ingenuity. Over the course it has turned hundreds of once naïve children into established young persons. The machine has tested each one of us, whether it be attitude, stamina or just academic ability, the machine was there – pushing each product to its limit, to make or break the victim. In primary school, there were so many limitations, from the school security to the general examinations, it was very much on the half empty side. I resembled a big fish in a little pond. But once entering secondary school. I was now surrounded by people in my position – people who were bigger, stronger and cleverer than myself. This all adds up as healthy competition, as without these other contestants I would most definitely not feel the urge to push for top spot, and would be complacent as the top dog, with nowhere to go but down. During school, you develop your character, and I certainly did. Learning more academically, developing my character, and learning to accept are all traits I picked up, and traits that that will cross your path unless you are too ignorant to look outside your own circle: the circle that is yourself, if you look outside the circle, outside the barriers, that is where you can learn to accept yourself. The mirror was invented to look at your image, not your soul. We can all look in the mirror and say how beautiful one is, but until we see ourselves, hear ourselves, from another's point of view, we cannot judge and accept ourselves, on our own opinions from our own eyes.

Today I can see the products of the laughter, the tears, the smiles and the fights I've endured and exploited during my five years at secondary school. Dating back to my first day at school, I was shy, nervous and naïve, now

I have become a lot more confident. This is through my experiences. You don't realize and understand things by just reading about them; sometimes you have to experience them and sometimes make mistakes to understand the intensity of situations and emotions. An element of naïvety is carried through 'till you reach death's door, even though many adults believe they grow out of naïvety when they finally reach maturity. I also like to remind myself and them, there's no fool like an old fool.

I think that since being entered into the daunting prospect of secondary education, I have learnt valuable skills for life, learning that life is not always what it seems, and experience is vital to the oasis, that is an experienced, fulfilled life. Relationships don't happen overnight, and this I also have learnt in secondary school. Relationships are one of man's most important discoveries, without them we would be living life as a single-minded being.

But now, as I'm facing the same prospect entering college, being shadowed by older students, I'm somewhat more convinced about the changeover than I was five years ago, secure in the knowledge that 'Big School' has taught me valuable morals and lessons that I will use and need in later life. As I look at my time. I have enjoyed it, but sadly it must draw to an end and I must make the most of the mistakes and misadventures I've stumbled across, and remark upon them as being instrumental in the making of me.

> *Wherever you roam*
> *And admit that the waters*
> *Around you have grown*
> *And accept it that soon*
> *You'll he drenched to the bone.*
> *If your time to you*
> *Is worth savin'*
> *Then you better start swimmin'*
> *Or you'll sink like a stone*
> *For the times they are a-changin*
>
> *Bob Dylan*

Josh Bartholomew

Becoming a Teacher

Everyone dreams of a celebrity lifestyle. I did. A while ago, however, I realized that in life, you need a lot of luck, and for that lifestyle, you need all the luck in the world.

I've always wanted to act. I like it when people applaud you and I love the feeling of knowing that the show just done had put a smile on everyone's faces.

But I don't want to keep this talent to myself; I want to teach it.

I envy teachers. They see you develop and they get the satisfaction of knowing that they have helped someone take a step, (and sometimes a leap) towards their dreams.

I want to feel that. I want children to look up to me and ask me questions, their faces full of determination and awe when you give them an answer.

I also want that feeling of power and authority for we all see teachers as people of strength and strictness. I want to feel that smug satisfaction of knowing that you can bring any disrespectful year eleven boy to shake at his knees.

Of course, I'll need to study for this life. As soon as I leave school, I'm rushing to college, then I shall rush to University, then I'll rush to teacher training. No gap year for me. I want to get my life sorted as soon as I can, for life is a precious thing and there's so much I want to see.

I'm not saying the rush is going to be a poor job! I can be a <u>very</u> committed person. As I said, life is precious, so I want to do as best as I can, for the dream job of pushing around people smaller than me is something I desperately want!

This is not something I want for my whole life; for I'm sure the novelty of telling off children must wear off after 15 years.

I want to travel the world after teaching. I've helped people all my life, now I'm going to help myself. I love exotic lands: India, China and the Caribbean will be my first destinations, for these places fascinate me.

While I am in Africa, I will relight my old pastime: teaching. I want to help those who are in need of a better life and it will be from the heart, unlike all those glamorous people who travel with a hound or flashing and clicking hyenas, watching their every move.

You may have realized that all my life I have been helping children; however, I have none of my own. This is where travelling ties in with my life.

I've always felt that it's a gift to have a child; however, it's even more of a gift if you know you're saving a child.

My Dream is to adopt, for again, the feeling of satisfaction from the teaching days will reoccur: knowing I have helped someone achieve a better life. Why bring a new child into the world, when there are thousands desperately waiting for a loving family?

I want my life to be eventful. People I know are stuck in mediocre lives which just repeat themselves every day, like a stuck record.

Of course our lives don't go exactly how we plan, however, if we try hard enough, the outline will be exactly how we want but the inside will be full of surprises.

I want to start living my dream and I know there will be fear, death, tears, breakups and accidents, however, these things are what make your life unique.

Chloe Crichton

The Dark Side

The dark side of the human imagination interested me ever since I was little: witches, warlocks, werewolves... It was all fascinating to me since about the age of four. But beyond all that, vampires were always my main focus. I don't know why I have always been fascinated by the darker side, but my mum is convinced that it all started because, as a little girl, I used to be scared of everything; strange shaped shadows and the darkness used to scare me a whole lot. This is when my parents decided to show me that there is nothing to be afraid of in the dark. But instead of just showing me around the room, they took me out for a walk at midnight. I loved it, and after that it became a frequent thing; especially in winter, when there was a lot of snow, me and my parents used to go out and play snowball fights and build snowmen at night.

I think I started liking vampires the first time I heard about them, in the movie called 'From Dusk Till Dawn'. The vampires shown there are the sort everyone is familiar with: afraid of crosses, burn when holy water is spilled on them, die when stabbed in the heart with a wooden spear... But over the past few years people generally lost interest in this sort of vampire. According to many, as well as myself, they are old fashioned and clichéd. The vampires that are more appealing to the audience now are those which Anne Rice writes about in her novels. They are beautiful (as depicted by Victoria Frances in many of her works), have once been human, and remember it, which gives the vampire 'race' a whole new feel, because it shows that vampires are not just a meaningless horror subject with endless killing, but creatures which have emotions, feelings and hopes; and they are not as easy to kill as one would think.

It is often the case, that when I share this complete and utter fascination with other people, I hear the question "do you believe vampires exist?" My short answer in this case is "No." But if I am asked to elaborate, I would say something like "No, but I wish they would." And it's true, because I don't know about you, but quite frankly, I like to let my imagination wander and wish that these majestic and mysteriously beautiful creatures would exist without anyone knowing, for this why this myth is so beautiful as well as frightening.

The myth itself originated in the Far East and was transported from places like China and Tibet to the Mediterranean. Here they spread out along the Black Sea coast to Greece, Balkans and the Carpathian Mountains, as well as Hungary and Transylvania. Because the myth is so well known all over the world, one could not expect it to be the same everywhere. We, Europeans, are very familiar with the vampire, Count Dracula: a male with fangs and a suave manner, who can also turn into a bat whenever he wants to. However, in some ancient Greek myths a vampire is very often associated with a female - half woman, half serpent who lives in caves, where she feeds off the blood of children. In African tribes a vampire is known as a monster, living in a forest which is very rarely seen, yet preys on unwary passers-by; he lets his hook-shaped feet dangle off the treetops where he sits and catches people with them. These are but a few examples of thousands of myths that exist all around the world.

However, European myths seem to be slightly more realistic. This is because they were loosely based on real people. For example, the myth of Count Dracula was based on Prince Vlad III Dracula who was born in 1431 and died in 1476. He was a prince of Wallachia, which is now a part of Romania. He became known as a vampire for his brutality and bloodthirstiness (for the same reasons he also attained a nickname Vlad the Impaler). As well as him, Countess Elizabeth Bathory is sometimes referred to as a vampire. She was a Hungarian countess, who was born in 1560 and died in 1614. She is seen as a vampire because she killed young ladies and bathed in their blood, for she believed that this would keep her preserved and young forever. This is also how she got her nicknames "The Blood Countess" and "Countess Dracula".

Only recently have people realized that vampires couldn't actually be real. During the middle Ages vampires were not only strongly believed in by the religious people, but they were also feared. People took precautions in order to not be attacked by vampires. When a relative died, it was not uncommon to put poppy seeds in the coffin before burying it in the sacred ground. This was because people used to believe that poppy seeds will keep the vampire occupied by counting them instead of preying on their relatives. It was also believed that having garlic on the table by the bed will keep you safe if a vampire would choose to attack you while you sleep, for the smell of garlic would keep the vampires away.

Of course, these beliefs have now been abandoned, and anyone who still does that nowadays is seen as a 'wacko' or a 'weirdo'.

Of course, it wouldn't be like me if I wouldn't have expressed my love for vampires in the poetry which I write. I have a few poems about these creatures, and even though they are mythical, when I express myself through poetry they come alive for me. I think this is not unlike when an author is writing a novel. Thus, I based my poem *"Murder is a Child's Game"* on the novel *"Interview with the Vampire"* by Anne Rice. My poem is about the vampire child – Claudia – a beautiful girl who never grows old. I also mention how she doesn't have many human feelings or morals because she was 'born' to the dark side as a little child, and didn't get to experience much of human life. This being different from the vampires who would have been 'born' to the dark side after they've lived at least 20 years, which would let them associate everything with human emotions, hopes and beliefs. But again, speaking like this will make you think I believe vampires are as real as you and me, and this, of course, is the last thing I want to do.

So, after all this I will let you decide for yourself whether you wish to regard vampires as a myth which evolved over many years, and still has a magnificent impact on the modern audience, or just as creatures of fiction, which are nothing more than creations of ever so brilliant human imagination.

Veronika Nekrasova

Why I Hate Lampposts

I loathe lampposts. I absolutely detest them. They're not just ugly, they're an eyesore. Not only are they ugly, but they pollute the world, or to put it another way, they pollute the skies. As well as all this, lampposts hide our stars from view, cause threats to wildlife, health problems, accidents, and the greenhouse effect. You may be thinking, how on earth could lampposts threaten wildlife? Or cause health problems? It sounds impossible, but it's true, as I will explain later.

The sky should be black at night, but as we've developed a 24 hour society, the natural order of things has been destroyed. Light pollution now hides nearly all our stars from view, so now it's difficult to spot even the brightest of stars. In most parts of the UK, all we are left with is a harsh orange glow which seems to rise from the horizon. I'm sure you've all seen it, maybe when you were being driven home on a clear night, or as you opened your bedroom window to let some air in.

The problems caused by light pollution are many. Animals get confused by all the new light and change their feeding and breeding patterns. People are being deprived of sleep as the night is being shortened. Accidents are occurring more frequently because drivers are being blinded by high level lighting and security flashlights. Light pollution is contributing to an increase in greenhouse gases.

But what has this got to do with lampposts? Lampposts are one of the biggest causes of light pollution; in fact, the average lamppost sends 30% of its light up into the sky, where it is lost forever. The energy used is equivalent to that produced by two generating stations, power that could run thousands upon thousands of houses across the country. Thankfully, more and more towns and cities are buying new, modern street lighting that only sends light down towards the pavement, where we need it most

My local lamppost, or to put it another way, the one right outside my front door, is a disgusting sight. Clamped to it, at head level is a grotty white sign, splattered with mud and dirt. The sign reads 'No fouling, keep dogs on lead', and to accompany this delightful slogan is a large picture of a dog and a turd. Unluckily for me, I get the pleasure of seeing it every morning on the way to school, and every afternoon as I return. Not a pleasant way to start the day.

The rest of my local lamppost isn't much better. Around the bottom there are huge rust marks were the silver paint has flaked off, plus stains where the local dogs have done their business. The top half is even worse. It is festooned with bird droppings that haven't been cleaned off for years. Some may even be older than me. It's impossible to see all these droppings from the pavement, so the only people who notice them are me and the other people in my house, as we look out of the bathroom window.

So lampposts pollute the world. They threaten wildlife, and cause health problems. But they are not all bad. They light our streets, they make the world a safer place... in general. I must admit, they can do good. To me, they are a necessary evil; both good and bad, there to help and hinder our world. They just need a 're-vamp'. A new, energy-efficient design. A more elegant posture. With time, lampposts could even become stylish and modern. Well, that's my dream.

But for now, lampposts aren't perfect. In fact, as I've just said, they need a lot of improvements. The amount of energy and light they waste is horrific. They hide our stars from view. They contribute to the greenhouse effect and global warming. That's why I hate lampposts, and that's why I've given this talk.

Claire Westrop

Chavs

Chavs. Where can I start? I suppose I should start with what they actually are. Technically speaking, they're human beings; however this can be debated. The only reason I have for this debate, if it were to happen, would be their behaviour. Not their anatomy, not their looks (well maybe) but their behaviour.

Three or four years ago, yobism and 'chavness' wasn't really a big deal, well not to me anyway. There was the occasional group of teenagers causing havoc, but not to the extremes that we read about today. If I am to be honest, I used to be one of those people, who didn't cause mayhem and trouble, but went out at night with big groups of friends dressed in weird tracksuit-type clothes. This is probably the reason I hadn't heard a great deal about these chavs before, smoking, drinking, doing drugs; I was friends with them. Fortunately for me, I severed my connections with them before the 'curse of the chav' got me.

After I annulled these friendships, whenever I saw a group of chavs, I tried to avoid them. Now I had heard these stories on the news of what they were starting to act like, my view of them changed and I became prone to prejudging everyone who wore tracksuits and went around in groups of 10+. I think a lot of people also started to have this problem. They see a group of teenagers and think back to the stories they've heard of an innocent man being brutally attacked by them for no reason. This makes people a little paranoid and they find themselves looking over their shoulders, just checking that these particular chavs aren't psychopaths coming over with knives. Anyway, these people were making me feel uneasy, and they hadn't even done anything yet.

I mentioned their looks in my opening paragraph, and I think everyone has become accustomed to how they dress. The common chav, in my view, is the worst: dirty tracksuit that they wear everyday; black trainers that they've had for years; baseball hat, again dirty, that covers the top of their long, greasy hair, but not the curly bit at the bottom. I could ask anyone to describe a common chav and the description will be very similar to the one I just gave. It's like they're all clones.

Gradually, as I got older, I came to realize that the majority of chavs are all talk. They get lairy, but that's it. For this reason, I didn't change my prejudices on them, but the way in which I handle them. Now, whenever

I pass a group of them, (usually at night, it's when they all seem to come out) I'm not worried about whether they're going to stab me or something, resulting in me crossing the road or taking similar action, I just walk straight past them, acting as though they're not there. They ignore me too, most of the time, but not always. These are the lairy ones trying to intimidate people. It's usually, "Got a fag mate, innit?" or, "Go in the shop for me." It's pathetic, not intimidating, and I now realize how lucky I was and how lucky I am that I'm not like them: dirty and hated by everyone.

Now we come onto the girl chavs. Groups of these girls have slowly crept up after the nationalization of male chavs. They are similar in behaviour, sometimes worse, sometimes better, and wear the same clothes as the boys, but sometimes in pink which I think looks stupid anyway. The only reason I see for them to exist is to even the equation. No ordinary female is going to want to be friends with a typical male chav, so these girl chavs were invented. They are there because no one else will be, and are as, antisocial and unpleasant as the male species is.

Now comes the big question: why do people become chavs? I personally don't know why anyone would want to be, but there are theories as to why. One theory is that you are born into it. If your parents are chavs, then so are you. Well, when you're old enough to hold a cigarette, then you are. This is probably true as everyone is aware of the influence that parents have on their children, so in a way, it is the parent who should be blamed for the behaviour of the child, if this theory were to be true. Another theory is that you become a chav in your early teens by being with other chavs. Peer pressure, maybe? If this is the case, then there is hope for most people out there that haven't chosen what social group to belong to. All you have to do is avoid them and you'll be fine.

Nowadays, I tend to refer to them as 'scum' and perhaps I shouldn't, but it's the way I feel and I can't help it. It doesn't help that they keep proving me right, but that's besides the point. As I said at the very beginning of my little rant about how my perception of chavs has changed in the years I've been putting up with them, technically they ARE human beings. If so, they are of the lowest form, even below Southampton fans, and I have now come to realize, and I think most other people have too, that the less you have to do with them, the better.

Alex Fletcher

Food

Food is a necessity which we all enjoy. Whether you put away takeaways on a weekly basis, or can barely stomach half a Tic-Tac to keep trim, we all have relationships with what we eat. By now you're possibly thinking that there must be something more important to talk about; why not discuss taxes, the government, immigration laws or terrorism? I personally feel we have heard just about enough of that. So I propose this question: what is this obsession with size double zero? Why is it our society chooses emaciation over obesity as a symbol of beauty? Both represent ill health, and yet it is a state of being that so many desire.

In our 'oh-so-perfect' society we use obese people as the target of taunts. Passing this statement off as "it's just him that thinks that" shows that you are in self-denial. Even the best of us has seen an unfortunately shaped person and thought "she clearly likes her food"; yet it seems very few of us stop and wonder if there could be other explanations, such as genetics, ill health or diabetes. Have we ever considered that being slightly overweight does not automatically make somebody unhealthy, unattractive or undisciplined in their alimentary consumption? In this article, I aim to inform people that being slightly overweight or underweight is not horrendously devastating or hauntingly tragic, but is just the way we were made and how we developed.

When I began researching the taboo on beauty and weight, I was baffled by how our opinions have changed in just a few centuries. In pagan cultures, an overweight woman was revered not only as a symbol of sanctity and lust, but of great significance to the human race; being slightly overweight meant they were more fertile, similar to the old English philosophy that a woman with naturally large breasts would bear healthy children. It's funny how what was once regarded as a symbol of fertility has become the symbol of someone who has indulged themselves with one too many McDonald's. This 'fancy for flab' in history progressed to the Mediaeval period, where obese women were painted in awe; this conception of beauty was called 'Rubenesque'.

It's perhaps 'tarring the whole of Britain with one brush' when I claim that the understanding today is quite the contrary. To my utmost horror, being stick-thin has become the denotation of beauty, particularly in the modelling industry. On Channel 4's documentary 'Superskinny vs. Supersize', a model claimed that the models' toilets at a fashion show were covered in sick and diarrhoea. But hey, it's really beautiful, right? I mean, having an eating disorder and starving yourself of essential minerals must be an attractive quality? To me, the whole concept sounds raving mad. I think we can all agree that taking a girl out on a date who orders "just a glass of water, please" is slightly unromantic. The only beneficial reason I can think of is that when it comes to food, she won't be burning a hole in your pocket

And don't just think it was in Europe that we put great emphasis on weight. In the North African country of Mauritania, it is common practice to feed up girls as young as seven with ridiculously fatty foods. These girls are often force-fed foods loaded with saturated fats and high-calorie yak milk; this was wittily referred to as 'wife-fattening farming' in the UK. This tradition, quite fortunately, is now often not seen as healthy, nor humane in a civilized society. In recent years, the frequency of this tradition has dropped to one in ten girls being 'farmed'. Now the beauty 'trend' in Mauritania is for women to be of average build. Not skinny, not ill, not weak.

The more I explored this topic of radical dieting and self-destruction, the more I found myself delving into the reasons why people turn to health-shattering compulsions such as anorexia nervosa and bulimia nervosa. At first thought, I was hasty to conclude that the only reason people turn to dangerous extremes like this is to get thin. It turned out I was mistaken. Many scientists studying human psychology have found that besides giving the patient a destructive 'drainage' of the body's necessary commodities, bulimia and anorexia (sometimes shortened to 'bulimarexia') give people what they believe to be self-control. I have no doubt that a set of mental and dietary strictures would teach people discipline through arduous 'tough love', but why would anybody use an eating disorder to gain control? Some anorexics and bulimics feel food is the only thing they have under their control in life: possibly a result of abuse, bullying or self-torment. The facts remain that anorexia and bulimia are not only life-threatening, but leave the victim ultimately very much out of control.

I personally enjoy my food, and am rather proud of this. I also do not understand those who say "I hate Chinese food" or "I can't stand Indian food." I view this as narrow-mindedness. I'm sure it is possible that you didn't enjoy the last Chinese you had, or the one before that, or even the one before that; it's not fair to suddenly deny your tastebuds the exploration of different cuisines, just because you didn't like the last meal you had. It's quite possible to enjoy toast, but hate baked beans. I like samosas, but can't stand bhajis. I love beef in oyster sauce, but abhor cuttlefish. I like cheese and onion crisps, but hold contempt for salt and vinegar. Yes to a meat feast pizza any time of day, but a vegetarian one I can easily turn away. I urge you now, to scrap your voluntary starvation, and eat: eat as much as you want, and enjoy it; just make sure you don't go overboard. Eating no breakfast, no lunch and no dinner may serve you well now, but when your skin frays, your hair falls out, and your organs rot, I'm sure the reflection in the mirror of your local hospital's toilet won't seem so glamorous.

Thomas Newman

Africa

Did you know that Africa is not a country? Well, that might sound like a ridiculous question to ask but from the impression I got when I first came to England this is a rather relevant question. I was in the classroom one day, and, as the new girl, some of the girls came around me and were asking me questions about life in Africa. Being the proud Zimbabwean I am, I began to tell them about my country. One of the girls then went on to ask me what the capital city of Africa is. I began to laugh as I thought she was trying to joke around or being sarcastic to one of the other girls. She wasn't laughing. That's when I realized that she was being serious.

I felt a bit infuriated by the stupidity that this girl displayed but I then came to realize that it was just simply ignorance and she is only one out of many. Africa is not a country. I felt that it was necessary to clear up the misconceptions that people have towards Africa as a continent and the individual countries it is made up of. One African cannot speak for the rest of the other Africans the way that one American can try to sum up what every American is thinking. All of the African countries are very unique in their own way and the only thing we all share is being in the same continent. I then began to tell her that Africa is not a country it is a continent made up of individual countries; the way that Europe is made up of various countries such as Italy, Spain and Norway. Yes, we do relate to each other as countries such as the war in Darfur but this does not mean that every country in Africa is at war. For example in my country there might be serious political and economic corruption but we are at peace! There is no war and not everyone is in the refugee camps. The typical fight in my country would he a man being beaten up because he jumped the line in a bank queue. Depending on how serious the fight is, this might even be shown on the six o'clock news. Someone does get killed once in a blue moon but it's very rare. Guns and bombs are somewhat 'alien weapons.' This is just as bad as it can get. We are all different. Africa is not a country.

The same girl then went on to ask me another question. She then asked. "So do you ever see lions in your back yard?" I got even more irritated as I thought I had knocked some sense into this girl's head. Clearly I hadn't. Feeling very annoyed I said "No!" very sharply. I then started to explain that within many different African countries there are game parks and reserve parks where all the wildlife is kept. Just like there are zoos in the Western world. You will not walk out into your backyard and see a

54

leopard lying in your garden. It's just not possible! Yes in some countries there is a lot of chaos where everything is everywhere but only in economic and political situations not in the organisation of habitats; at least I know this is so in my country. People will queue for fuel, bread, money and even cooking oil. In some countries this is what to expect but not every country is like this. In some areas there is no electricity and some would be lucky to have the supply at least twice in a week. Water is another problem. Yes, we need cleaner water in Africa. God knows how many potholes my mother's car has hit in the road. People need to understand that 'ghetto' is not a state of mind, it's a situation and no one wants to be in the 'ghetto.' The media show little half-naked children dying of hunger and disease in Somalia or Ethiopia and the main heading usually consists of the word 'Africa.' From this, the viewers begin to think that there are little children dying of hunger and disease in Africa; the whole of Africa. I feel like I have to re-emphasize the point that Africa is not a country. Yes there are children dying of hunger and disease in Africa but this is only in some parts of Africa. The media clearly is not doing a very good job in letting people know what Africa is like. They have an influence on their viewers to 'stereotype' life in Africa.

Africa is considered to be a 'Third World' but this does not mean that we do not have half the facilities people have in the Western world or as they like to call it the 'First World.' This naming only promotes segregation because it leads to stereotyping. In Africa we have most of the services they have in the Western world. In my country, for example, we have shopping malls, televisions, radios, Internet, black Hummers, white Chryslers, silver limos... We have most of the things they have in the west. The media portrays Africa to be the poorest place in the world that is in desperate measures and this is what infuriates me the most. I think that the media should stop doing this and start informing the viewers on how they can stop such injustice in the world. Everyone is equal and I don't believe in class. We are all the same but still different in our own little ways. We can only help each other to make the world a better place.

Despite all these flaws, I think that Africa is the most beautiful place known to mankind. We might not have the technology that you may find in the United Kingdom or in America but I guarantee you that most African countries are trying to improve their infrastructure. Africa is yet to be one of the leading continents in this entire planet. Everything needs time to grow and develop and after Africa has gone through this, people are yet to enjoy its pleasures. I'll give one example: there is a vast amount of land and space. Whereas in Europe, it is too crowded and there are small 'flats' to rent which barely have a backyard for the whole of my family to congregate. The average house in my country is at least on a two and a half acre plot of land – usually with a swimming pool and gazebo in the back yard.

Africa is harmless to our world today. Statistics show that Africa produces less pollution than the western countries. Bombs and terrorists are also 'aliens' to us. Why then do people look down on Africa? We are not all at peace but most of us are. Who is at peace; a half-naked African child starving or an American teenager at fear of going to school because the boy he sits next to him threatened to bring in a gun and shoot him?

Africa has its differences as a continent and as the individual countries it is made up of. I think we deserve a better understanding and rating in our world today. So much potential lies within us and yet it is not recognized because the other western countries have not worked on making it a better place. If we all work together, not only as a continent but as an entire planet, we could be talking otherwise.

Sandra Mayenda

Body Piercing

Each and every human has preferences, most for influential and recognized reasons. I, however, have a fascination with body modification, mainly piercing. Odd, is a word that may spring to mind; surely your classic blonde hair, blue eyed, female, 15 year old would indulge in hair straighteners, or make up? Perhaps the opposite sex, or shoes? While others anticipate the monthly clothes shopping trip, I'm still deciding where else I could possibly jab an earring. I ask you, broaden your narrow mind for I am neither an 'emo' nor do I wear black on a daily basis. I proudly enjoy the elegance of ballet and wallow in the plaudits of performing arts.

At four years old, my mother took me to Plymouth market to have my ears pierced. After hearing the beautiful click of the piercing gun and screaming in pain, I was bribed to silence with a Mr. Whippy ice cream, while the two tiny studs in my ears sparkled gently in the sunshine. Of course, my enthrallment with B.M did not begin to unfold till many years later, on my 13th birthday. After many pleas and "if-god-wanted-extra-holes-in-your-body-he-would-have-put-them-there"s, my father caved in. Walking into the parlour, I felt the now-familiar butterflies and adrenaline beginning to pump through my veins. The moment I met the artist, clad with countless studs and tattoos, was the very moment I consider to be the beginning of my fascination. She looked striking, so unique. Instantly, I felt a burning desire to look like her, I wanted desperately to show off a pair of gleaming ears.

I have never favoured a piercing that I haven't then got done, the running total: 10. My ears alone have 8, the list being first and second holes, helix, orbital, tragus and scaffold. And while facial piercing doesn't always float my boat, my newest addition is a nose stud. Yes, I shamelessly hold my hands up, I've bonded with my modifications in such a way my anxiety levels soar if I notice I'm missing a earring. They've become a part of me you see...

And so I sat and smiled when the woman at the hairdressers had tried coaxing me to take my piercings out, telling me that I'd look ridiculous as an elderly lady. She had been horrified at the sight the long metal bar poking through the top of my right ear. I couldn't see what on earth was wrong with it, and as her colleagues crowded round staring as if I was an extra terrestrial, I felt a pride in the fact that I was looked upon as being different. It was on this day, after being faced with the question "what made you want that?", that I realized my fixation with piercing had no reason to be there, I for once, could not answer back.

I do much wonder, why I attracted the women that day; are piercings becoming more socially unacceptable? Ok, so what about tattoos? They are the second most common form of B.M, and yet not many will bat an eyelid at the sight of a little ink. A view I like to take, and I'm not particularly religious, is that God the creator, made us as blank canvasses. He then gave us the originality and the equipment to decorate our canvas, in whatever way we like. Some are simply afraid to break the norm, as H.L Mencken once said: "The average man does not want to be free. He simply wants to be safe." The compelling interest is fuelled by these words, you only have one body and one life, why play everything safely? I feel that it gives a person an undoubted edge, they're taking a risk, why aren't you? In the same way someone would dye their hair or apply make up, others choose to modify their bodies in a more permanent way.

And so finally... to all of those stops and stares, those mutters under your breath, my vivid attraction with B.M remains and will continue. I'm going to brighten up my blank canvas; if you don't like it, look somewhere else!

Megan Holland

Oranges and Lemons

What am I?

It is an illuminous moon rising gently in the east. It
is a tennis ball and has rough pith. It has a rough
stalk at the top which looks very much like a
button.

As you cut me through the middle it is like blood
dripping from a body. My juice pours from my
centre. It smells very strong and glistens.

It tastes very sour and sweet. It has a centre that is
white and looks like a caterpillar. What am I?
Can you guess?

Alfie Steeves

What is it?

It is a bright sun rising over the bright blue sea,
a tennis ball punching the air, fighting to get to the
racket first
with a lizard skin coat to keep it warm.

It has the feel of a rough road leading into the
deserts of Africa and the smell of orchards in May
It looks like a piece of flint chopped in half by
huge boulders

The feel of a hundred feather beds and
The taste of a million tiny electric shocks running
Down your spine

Sarah Allen

Sherbet Lemon

When you first set your eyes on sherbet lemons they look so
smooth and shiny.

They are as yellow as a ripe banana.
The shiny wrapper gently reflects the light.
When you unwrap the sweet it makes a crack and a clatter
when you drop it on the table.

When you smell, you can smell the sweetness and the sour.

When you touch the sherbet lemon it's smooth
like glass. But in other parts it's rough like an old
piece of wood.

As soon as you put the sherbet lemon in your mouth straight
away you taste the sourness but all of the sudden too sweet.

As soon as you crack into it the sugar slides out of the sherbet
lemon. You wish for it to never end.

Alex Henton

Sizzling Sherbet
and
Lovely Lemon

A fluorescent sunflower,
Shiny and smooth,
As if it were blowing in the wind,
Its wrapper reflected in the sun.
It feels crackly, as crunchy as a bowl of Crunchy Nut
cornflakes on a stressful Monday morning.
Delicate and light,
As light as feather falling from the sky,
But when landing crashes loudly on the ground.
Fizzing in the sun,
Sour and sugary,
Glued to the top of my numb mouth,
Slowly it starts to dissolve.
My face screwed up like a shrivelled prune.
Only few words to describe it:
Sugary, Zesty, Succulent and Sour.

Lillie Boyett

Sour but Sharp

Do not touch its hard outside
the waxy, succulent, gritty skin
will peel your mind into the zesty surrounding
but do not swallow its sting taste
its burning sensation will kill you.

The sour wheel of spinning death
Will not be there for ever the
Opaque inside will burst into a
Thousand drops of blood its burning
Sensation will kill you.

As fragile as it is; it's as
Hard as a stone do not
Trust in its sweet lying taste
Because the powerful juices
Will rise and its burning sensation
Will kill you.

By Taya Collings-Bush

The Innocent Trap

Juice imprisoned in a waxy cage.
As reflecting as a mirror.
It is rugby ball shaped.
The surface shines like the sun.

When the juice is released the cut looks opaque.
Its fragile appearance shall trick you.
It gleams and glistens in the sunshine.
It looks innocent and honest.

The smell is zingy and zesty.
Its power and ferociousness is surprising.
It shall trick you to taking the first bite.
BIG MISTAKE.

Lara Cooper-Chadwick

Oranges

I am a golden moon, shining brightly across the horizon.
People staring at me in the sky, from all around.
I look like a tennis ball, until you get close,
I do not bounce, but if you dropped me I will go SPLAT!!
I rock from side to side, like boats on the rocky waves.
I feel lumpy, but smooth
Circular and oval
Glowing and shining, through the day.
I taste sharp and sour
But sweet and succulent
You can't resist me, all slimy and juicy
Just sitting there, in the fruit bowl.

Charlotte Brown

Remembrance

Where was he?

Where was he the day ...
The simplicity of living was stolen?
Where was he when the vulnerability of childhood was violated?
Where was he when murder had justification?
Where was he when innocence was shattered by power?
Where was he?

Where was he the day ...
The dream of divine intervention became meaningless?
Where was he when the vanity of man was exploited?
Where was he when diversity was tainted?
Where was he when the flaw in human nature became abominable?
Where was he?

Where was he the day.
The stench of rotting flesh became unbearable?
Where was he when individuality became persecution?
Where was he when the last spark of hope went out?
Where was he when the feeling of abandonment was overwhelming?
Where was he?

Where was he the day ...
The evil of power seemed invincible?
Where was he when exclusiveness became a humble hope?
Where was he when guilt went unrecognized and became a blind emotion?
Where was he when there was nowhere to run and nowhere to hide?
Where was he when my individuality became abnormality?
And I ask myself, where was he? Where was he?
I ask again, where was he?

Right beside me.

Candice McKechnie

The Sheltering Shade of a Tree

The sheltering shade of a tree
Calling to the small bird.
Its beauty ardent, its wings
A distant shiver, its peaceful singing
Heaven sent.

He is the snow on the bird's lips
The freezing taste,
The silvery sip. He is the breath on the bird's hair
Its endless nightmare in this
Devil's lair.

The bird knows not the emotions of
Hatred or of fear.
Free in his innocence he sheds
Not a tear. It knows not
The power of a moment of
Insanity or that his corpse
Will become part of that man's vanity.

The snow falls silently on
The cold winter's morning,
The silence only broken by the
Bird's peaceful singing. It wonders
Not why he has been brought to this
Desolate place but
continues its joyous singing.

The bird sees not how its mother cries
And the bird sees not the
Red demon's eyes.
The bird hears not the deafening din of
The western battle or how the red
Demon laughs at his mother's death rattle.

Aaron Spraggs

What's It Like, To Be A Mockingbird?

It's like fighting a losing battle,
No one seems to want to know,
I'm really an innocent old lady in her chair,
Rocking gently to and fro.

It's like a struggling tiger captured in a zoo,
I long to be wild and free,
No one watching for fun or laughter,
I'd be real, unique. I'd be me.

I'm like those calm rolling waves,
Lapping gently up onto the shore,
I'm their thoughtless piece of scandal,
Stripped of my identity and core.

It's like a harmless child thrown against a wall,
Or a lost butterfly, floating helplessly around a cemetery.
I want to break free from their prejudice,
And scrape the fake life I live from my memory.

It's like an enigmatic puzzle,
If you think hard enough you find,
A person you knew long before they talked,
I'm generous, cheerful, kind.

Megan Holland

The Poppy's Poem

You see the beauty of the poppy field,
you look up and expect to see a beautiful day,
but instead you see a dreaded, horrible war,
fought upon a most relaxed place.

You wonder why such beauty should be destroyed by two armies,
both sides forced to fight each other.
Misery created amongst a field of peace and love.

You see the blood of fallen soldiers
camouflaged amongst the redness of a wonderful flower.
You start to believe that maybe the flowers aren't so beautiful
if they match the horrors of war.

Bodies falling to the ground
like a petal on an autumn day.
You see beauty in this terror
and you begin to hate the war's continuous fighting.

Love, peace and beauty.
Slowly destroyed by the evil of the machines of war.
The weapons of destruction destroy everything in their path
for someone else's gain.

The colours blooming outwards
towards the death of many people
who did not choose to fight this war.
You are dragged into the chaotic war of a bloodthirsty army,
their path, chosen by another's greed.

The time of war ticks away
like a petal falling to the ground,
but the dying of the army does not stop, where as the petal
died a long time ago.

You see the dead bodies lying on the field
and the alive above them still fighting for a moment's peace,
to bury the dead who don't deserve to be left to rot.

You hate being attracted to the battlefield
which has both beauty and hatred in the most chaotic time.

You hope the war will stop; both sides stop the killing
they do
not want to bring upon another's life.

The colours have drawn you in too far,
and now you have reached the centre of a flower
with a black hole in the middle.
This is where you meet your death.
This is the war of the poppy.

Joseph Holman

Remember

Rows of poppies blow in the wind
Each one symbolizing a soldier
Each one symbolizing an unnecessary death
The eyes of courage.

He stood strong at guard
Machine gun loaded
Ready to battle.
The shot of a gun
Running cold through my ears.

The poppy's heart
An ebony interior
The deep, dark depression
Everlasting
Shining through every smile.

He's scared
It's visible
Yet understandable
He stops his tears
Yet inside he's dying.

Red and delicate they lay
Silent but meaningful
Shining through the months
Funny,
how it has an impossibility to utter a single word
Yet it speaks so much.

He watches his friends die
But he can't help them,
Save them.
Any hopes of surviving the war
Diminished from reality
Now nothing but impossible dreams.

Strong red colour represents
Everything they knew in the war.
Blood spilling everywhere
Though no time for tears.

Among the dying young
He stands surviving it all,
Watching them fall one by one
The empathy once received now fading

A poppy centre
A pair of crying eyes
A distraught family broken by war
A million men who died too young.

For those few minutes he gets to himself
He contemplates the past
The friends he loved and lost
And the future he dreads to live.

That lone poppy resting on his coffin
Stands out amongst the roses
One raindrop glistening on its petals
Representing a million tears shed.

Katy Gearing

Never Forget but Always FORGIVE....

The eye-catching allure
Of
The sickly stench of those sweet bloody bodies.

But of course this must be the distinctive view of no-man's land.

The strong piercing pain of death,
Haunts,
Haunts those in need of remembrance.

Those who were involved in the ever changing graphic images of war.

Deep down, forever inside the poppies exist,
The
Silent stillness of war.

The lives lost, grasped by hell's red and black cloak.

In all those levels and layers of war,
The
Outline of soldiers is defined and they are linked arm in arm.

All that drama is gone, shrivelled on Mother Nature's home.

The divine redness glowing at us as,
A
Sure sign of hope.

Lighting the path of success of glory and honour.

Today is the day we shall
Honour,
We shall link arm in arm and remember.

Today is the day we remember and we forgive.

Nicole Smith

To Kill a Mockingbird

1) Why is it a sin to kill a mockingbird?

2) Does he still sing after being sinned against?

3) Does the generosity continue after the song has ended?

4) Were the delicate souls enlightened by sin?

5) Was it their innocence that became the inspiration for others?

1) The beauty within a wave washing over the
Seabed as the mockingbird hums a desolate tune.
Perhaps knowing that sin
Will one day kill us all.

2) The soothing comfort from above still forgiving.
The red rose resting, lonely fading fast.
End is inevitable.

3) Living for the happiness of others,
The insignificant being soulfully walks the plank,
Hoping and praying for the
End of the rainbow.

4) The dove soars through the sky.
The tranquil air filled with voices
Of years gone by.
Lessons preached
By people of the past.

5) It is not remembered. Remember
The first-born baby bringing gleaming smiles
To every face. The lamb taking the first steps to
Freedom, the swan, head held high, showing passers by
Of what the future holds.
The sun smiles
And the clouds disappear.
Who can say? Innocence is now.

Katie Jackson

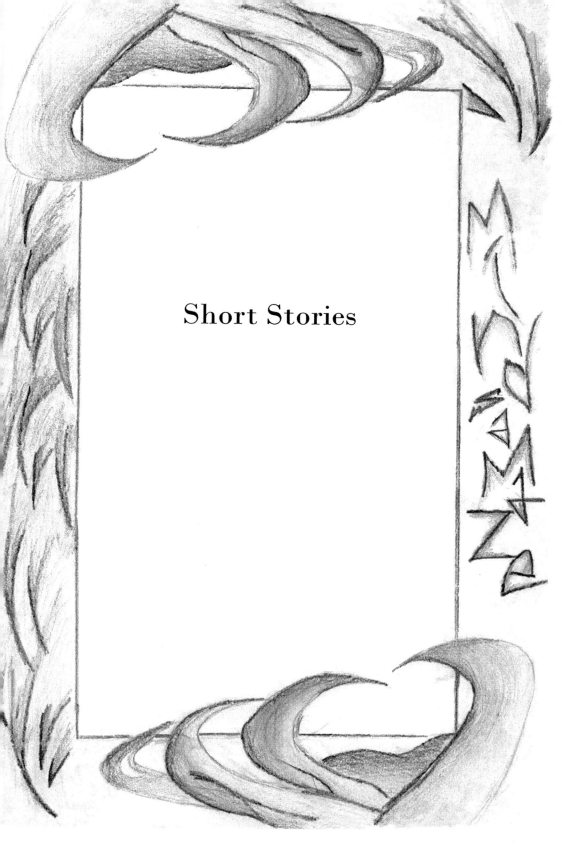

Short Stories

When the sunshine left Rosie's life

The little girl skipped along the road smiling sunnily up at her father who clasped her hand lovingly. She wasn't aware of the lines of worry etched on his familiar face, to Rosie the world was perfect: she was with her beloved Daddy; she was going to the park and she had been promised an ice cream with a flake!

The park was bright with flowers full of the sounds of summer; the laughter of children and the singing of birds. Rosie sat on the swing giggling "Higher, higher Daddy".

Mummy always said "no darling, that's high enough" but Daddy obligingly pushed harder. His thoughts were elsewhere, but Rosie didn't know that today was to be her last day of her idyllic childhood. The last day before a tsunami of worry and concern would flood her life.

The phone cheeped cheerfully from Daddy's pocket with the Tweenie theme tune Rosie had insisted on and had caused her father so much embarrassment. The swing gradually slowed as her father listened intently his face clouding over and his hand shaking. Suddenly he grabbed Rosie off the swing and started to run clumsily towards the gates of the park.

"Daddy. Ice cream, ice cream!" she sobbed but for the first time in her short life he ignored her as he rushed towards the car parked at the end of the sun-baked road. Quickly strapping her in her seat he gruffly said "Sorry sweetheart, Mummy's had to go to hospital, Granny is going to play with you."

The drive flashed by and the car screeched to a halt outside Rosie's Granny's house. Granny was standing on the pavement anxiously looking out for them. She leant in the back seat and grabbed Rosie, "phone me when you have some news" she pleaded and the car roared off without Daddy giving Rosie so much as a wave. Hours passed slowly, Rosie was aware that the silent phone had more of her Gran's attention than she did. They did jigsaws, sang songs and eventually Rosie snuggled down on the sofa for a nap her thumb comfortingly in her mouth, her face relaxed and babyish.

She didn't hear the phone eventually ring and her Gran crying quietly. She did not see her father's despairing face when he returned. She did not hear the tragic account of her mother's death as her baby brother fought his way into the world only to take a few breaths and die. When she woke her life was empty of joy, her mother would never again sing her a lullaby, plait her hair or kiss a poorly knee better and her father's face would never again be carefree and joyous.

When the next day dawned the sky was bright but the sunshine had left Rosie's life.

Sara Hopes

Diary

It had been a year ago, the day the waves had come, a day that will stay with me forever. Lurking, like the monster itself, deceiving and dangerous, showing no distinction. Old or young, rich or poor, everybody's lives were affected. My life transformed. Here is my story...

As I stepped off the boat, the sun crept over me illuminating the stunning island. The blue ocean, so elegant in its movements, was at one with the island; quite unlike England where its jerky movements were killers, dictating and destroying.

Sri Lanka was another world, I felt as if Mum, Dad, little Harry and I were like a normal family. Dad wouldn't have to scurry off to the office and mum wasn't off at any 'important gala'. Just the four of us, together. Although it may surprise some, the feeling was quite unknown to me.

I knew that Gran would have loved going to somewhere as far and exotic as Sri Lanka, she would have loved sipping those colourful cocktails given on arrival and of course, swimming with the dolphins. I wanted her to be there, with me. I remember her putting me to sleep when I was a child; she always used to say "Night Night Helen Melon". Rather stupid, isn't it? But surprisingly whenever I was ill or upset as a child, it was always her who I wanted. Her velvet tones were enough to make even the quietest feel happy and loved. Gran used to say, "If you're happy, you have everything, and nothing can ever take it away from you". She used to hate it when Dad flashed his money around, but that never stopped him doing so. He used to think money could buy anything and everything, but now I know he realizes money means nothing.

We arrived only a day short of Jesus' birthday, everybody's favourite festival. Christmas 2004 was going to be amazing, hours before the big day; don't ask me how, but I could even smell the aroma of tantalizing turkey tickling my taste buds.

That night, as I slept I could hear the delicate movements of the waves, softly gliding over the granules of sand as if it were protecting it. The moon was a light bulb, slowly lighting as the sun waded its way into the spotlight.

I remember Harry waking us all up, "It's Christmas!" he exclaimed, "Christmas! Christmas! Christmas!" After opening presents, we indulged in a full breakfast. Not a single soul in the dining area looked glum, the excitement of the day to come enticed even the most stern looking. Back then, nobody knew of what was to come, how could they? In their eyes, they would be having an exceptional, unforgettable time away; being smothered in the lap of luxury was, I'm sure, enough to take the insecurities away from anybody.

As the sun set, the mood particularly boosted, the sound of "Rockin' around the Christmas Tree" enticed my ears into swaying with the rhythmic beat. The pure beauty of the island astonished me, it was safe, the people were friendly and people's troubles seemed to just float away, drifting further and further into the unknown. As the evening drew on, I began to think of the people outside the hotel, what would they be doing on the much-loved occasion? Would they be pampered and cared for with oodles of attention?

The night drew on, Mum and Dad actually seemed to be enjoying each other's company, a feeling of contentment shot through my body – this was what life was really about: being happy. As the clock struck twelve, most of the attendees sauntered off to their villas, my family being one of them, unaware of the reality that was to come. A reality so awful it's still too real to comprehend, the events that followed will stay with me forever, haunting, lingering and poignant.

I was a grain of sand, waves washing over me, scrubbing at me, trying to erase or eradicate. The water furious, no longer gentle, still and calm.

The sun rose like it did on any normal day, bright and somewhat false, giving the impression that the day was as rosy as any another. I could already hear the banter of people going for their early morning jog. Harry and I awoke early excited and eager to spend the day around the pool. Lounging about with Mum and Dad seemed so insignificant to some, but for me, it was the only time I was able to spend time with them, without them thinking about work.

We were all set and ready to make for the sun, sea and sand. The resort was oozing with scrumptious smells, tantalizing tastes and soulful sounds. Everybody was so alive, to this day I still remember what the hotel looked like, how can I ever forget?

"Anyone want an ice cream?" I recall saying to Harry.

"Yeah, Vanilla please, and with lots of trickling strawberry sauce!"

I scurried over the packed beach, and placed myself in the never-ending queue. Just as my turn came, I felt a hand, persistent, and vexed, shaking me, warning me. I turned.

A monster of the sea leapt up, cascading and pounding at the unwary water. Then screams. Screams of terror. Screams of death.

A creature of the sea rose, engulfing anything in its way. It would show no mercy. Stripping. Destroying. Dictating.

On intuition, I knew that I had to reach high land. I had to get away. It was coming. Further and further never diminishing in its alacrity. People screeched all around me, trying to find their loved ones, trying not to be swallowed by the wave. My heart: pumping. My legs: jelly. Cries of terror entered my ears yet images of my family acted as fuel and encouraged me to flee.

No words could even begin to comprehend how I felt at that moment. What was I to do? Was I going to survive?

Tremors bounced under the granules of sand, decelerating my attempts to move. I wasn't going to win this fight. The opposition was stronger. The opposition – a killer. Only a mere fifty metres separated it from the crowds of people, I needed to seek refuge.

A tree? A car? A boat? Where was I to go? People clung onto anything. Anything they could find; entrepreneurs and locals alike gripped tightly, packed together; trying to resist.

It was already half way up the shore. The immense monster lifted its wings and sucked everything in its proximity; children and adults alike swallowed by the monster of the sea. Their lives snatched away in an instant, with no thought. Possessions and sentiments no longer mine but possessed by the superior, like a bully snatching your favourite toy.

I clung onto a tree, with all my might. Nothing was going to make me loosen my grip. Nothing. My thoughts flickered back to my family; although I couldn't concentrate on them too hard. Tears trickled down my anxious face yet my body wouldn't allow me to dwell on my emotions.

Twenty metres. Ten metres. Five metres. This was it. The giant hurled, crashing ferociously against everything in sight. Sweeping in its hurried motions, then dragging crumbling pieces and possessions back into its den. The wave was an epitome of death. People as well as possessions snatched away, stolen from their rightful place.

It came back for more. The wave boosted across, viciously seeking its prey. Remains of tables and chairs whizzed past me, floating as if travelling to no particular destination. My hands, weary and injured, had had enough however I could not let that feeling overtake. More than half my body was under its grasp.

Families next to me, wiped off in an instant, no longer enjoying the life they had once loved, but dragged into the unknown. The sound of mothers weeping clenched into my eardrums. Please, not my mother I thought to myself. Young children, mystified and afraid; grabbed onto the remains of tables, igniting unknown courage from within.

It was still coming, stronger than ever. My tree was slowly weakening. I could feel it. The monster was evidently jeering at it forcing it to back down. It was pulling back like an animal with its prey, dragging it back down along the once elegant seabed. Dead bodies floated around, expressionless and bewildered. Mine was going to be one of them, if I didn't act fast. My body; slowly becoming more of a victim, slowly weakening, slowly losing to the opposition.

"Help, Help, Help, Help!" I screamed at the top of my voice.

My screeches grabbed the attention of a local family nearby. I extended my hand, hoping incessantly for somebody to take pity.

"Please, P-p-please".

You could tell that they were poor. Their clothes were stained and their bodies skinny because of malnutrition. Yet, almost magically, my pleas worked. It was the father. It was the father who pulled me onto the safe surface of a once upper-class dining table. We wrestled the ground, hoping to nest in it, wishing to be able to stay for a few minutes longer.

The monster of the sea began to rear back. It had had enough for today. It had ruined enough lives for the time being. Crunching and crashing sounds filled my ears. For a moment, I even thought I was dead. I was frozen in my motions, memories of the land before haunted me.

Desolation and despair filled all around me while memories of my family resided in my brain. The land was unknown to me, rubble and furniture were scattered around. Bodies left to rot, left for families to mourn upon. Buildings crumbled to the ground. No longer was Sri Lanka that inviting place it once had been.

The stench of death diffused through the air. The expressions of the dead clambered through people's minds. Slowly, people started to move. The crying never stopped though. I remember a mother, weeping with sorrow in her loneliness; grabbing on to what was left of her son. She was alone. Everybody was alone. The presence of a God disappeared. How could such a God allow catastrophes like this to happen?

To this day, I've never seen so many people look as devastated. The Tsunami has taken away the little sense of happiness people had. Happiness that had been rightly theirs, but snatched away as if it was a possession of the monster. As were their homes, their families and lives; no longer a commodity but a privilege.

The hope of life had been sucked away from the lonely souls in sight. What was there without family? As I clambered on, amongst the rubble and debris, I almost didn't want to see my family; fears within me grew as I took each step further, into the unknown.

The water had calmed down; it was deceitful and in my eyes, gave the impression of a hidden character. On the outside, it looked beautiful and radiant yet underneath the surface there was rage of the likes no human could ever understand.

Concrete and bricks lay scattered, breaking the barrier between land and sea. The monster's victims lay restlessly, their bodies pale from astonishment and reeking of death

I heard whistles. A diminutive spark of hope flickered from inside however I tried not to keep my hopes up. Obviously, the hotel was reduced to mere rubble so I had to try and find my way back. The image through my eyes was worse than no man's land, no child should ever have to see what I saw.

Slowly, I could make out a half broken sign saying 'Eden Resort'. I was there. My entire life depended on the truth not disguised or concealed but a pure truth of despair or ecstasy.

I approached the swimming area – it was unrecognizable. Remains of sun beds were plonked on top of each other. The pool was partially derelict.

Families sat, huddled together, reliving the nightmare in their heads, over and over again.

"Mum? Dad? Harry?"

No answer. I carried on, "Mum-m-m?" this time my pitch increased, and as it did so, I grew more aware of the fact that I was a child, dependent and nurtured by my family and my deepest and most desperate desire, a desire to be reunited with my family may not be met.

I searched. I searched until my body couldn't take me any further. It was only about midday by then. We should have all been playing together, enjoying our time together, as a family. Instead, I was forlorn in a country that was not my own and alien to me.

Time passed gradually and I was nearly at the end of the lines of families that the monster didn't manage to swallow. Hollowness and emptiness filled their eyes, defeated and overcome by the colossal ogre concealed by the sea. My eyes resisting my surrounding conditions, shining and radiating minute hope that my family were alive. My eyes fell on familiar faces. It was her.

Her face broke into a smile that almost looked prohibited in the appalling state of affairs. My dad's eyes swallowed, consumed by emptiness, relief and grief, reached mine and I didn't need to ask. It was final. Absolute and irreversible. Nevertheless I asked: "Where's Harry?" Her face clouded.

Never have I seen my mother as helpless than at that moment. I could tell she was trying to stay strong but at that moment I knew her insides were ripping out with fear and anxiety.

We both knew, yet none of us had the courage to say it. Our eyes met for a split second. He was gone. An uncontrollable urge of despondency leapt from within me. I'd always been used to getting what I wanted, when I wanted. Now, I knew that no matter what was said or done, nobody could ever fulfil my desire.

Not a single day passes when I don't think of Harry. He was seven years of age, defenceless and unaware, when he breathed his last breath. He had experienced only seven years of joy and sadness alike, his life was not meant to be over yet, not then.

It hit Dad the hardest most, he learnt a huge lesson. He too learnt it the hard way. There were no more "Father and Son days out", no more, playing football in the park. Nothing.

Now, a year on, I still get nightmares; I hear his voice and the misery I experienced leaps back into my mind, haunting. Sometimes I even wish it was me who was lying at the bottom of the seabed. Sometimes I don't want to wake up in the morning, I don't want to see the next day.

The world can be a cruel place; you never know what life's going to throw at you, so that's why I appeal to you, the public. A year later, and there are still people living in poverty as a result of the disastrous attack. My brother is not here today but please; give others the chance of rebuilding their lives.

Serena Hathi

The Last Day

Today I walk with a spring in my step. Today is the day I have been waiting for so long. The last day of school. Just one more day and I'll be free for six whole weeks. Six weeks of freedom before I have to endure another gruelling year of school. But I don't think about that. All I can think about is all the fun me and my friends are going to have. A great bubble of happiness seems to be swelling inside me and I feel as if nothing can burst it.

The weather seems to be matching my mood. The blue sky illuminates the white houses, which seem to glow. I feel the warmth of the early morning sun tingling pleasantly on the back of my neck. I can hear birds singing tunefully around me, they too, enjoying the good weather.

It is only a ten-minute walk to the bus stop but I let it drag, delaying the moment I have to get inside.

As I turn the corner I can feel my phone vibrating in my jeans pocket. I flip it open and I can hear my mum shouting at me. I left my school bag at home, which is a frequent occurrence. The bubble inside me seems to shrink slightly, but I won't let something this small ruin today.

As I turn around to head home I can see a man staring at me. He has cold, steely eyes that send a shiver down my spine. I smile at him pleasantly and make my way home. I get a bit nervous but I try not to worry, we get a lot of weirdoes in this town.

I look up and I can see a few white clouds floating across the once clear sky. I hope the weather doesn't change, I'm enjoying this good weather.

The streets are quiet apart from the jingling coming from my purse. My friends and I are going out after school to celebrate, maybe go shopping or get a pizza. I have taken way more money than I need, but I've just had my birthday so I have plenty of money to spend.

As I round the corner of my road I can see the strange man again, staring at me like before, with his hands in his dark Adidas jacket pockets. When he sees me looking at him he leers at me, then turns around and tramps away, back into an alley. I sigh with relief and walk down the road.

I hope my mum isn't too angry when I... I feel something cold on my neck. I freeze.

"Hello sweetheart, why don't you be a good girl and jump in the car for me."

It's the cold-eyed man, he must have followed me from the alley. His face is right near mine. His breath smells terribly, and I can see only a few remaining teeth lying on top of rotting gums, all of which were almost black.

When I don't respond he moves the knife, which he is holding into the flesh of my neck, getting deeper and deeper until a trickle of blood runs down onto my shirt. The bubble inside me bursts as I realize the true danger that I am in.

I look at the car he is pointing at and then reach for the handle. The man smiles, his face still next to mine. I feel sick as his beard brushes against my cheek, and begin the shiver uncontrollably. I step into the car and sit down on the tattered leather seats. The last thing I see as he shuts the door is the grey clouds gradually travelling towards us.

We drive slowly through the town, as if not to draw attention to ourselves. I'm still shaking, but I breathe in deeply. I try to calm myself down and assure myself that everything will be OK, but deep down I know I'm in really serious trouble.

Soon I start crying uncontrollably, I try to steady myself but the tears won't stop coming.

"Just shut up and stop crying or I'll kill you!"

My phone begins to ring. I think it is my mum trying to see where I am.

"Turn it off."

I reach for my phone and switch it off, wishing with all my heart that I were home.

I can see that the man is apprehensive. His hands are shaking on the wheel.

We finally reach a rundown house at the centre of town, an area I generally prefer not to go to. He gets out of the car and shuffles to my door. All I want to do is lash out at him and run away, but I don't know what he will do to me if he catches me. He opens the door and sticks out his hand, trying to snatch at my arm. I spit at him and start punching him as hard as I can. My feeble blows don't seem to hurt him but I can see that he is really annoyed.

He snatches my arm and drags me out of the car. I fall on the pavement painfully on my right shoulder. I stand up, thinking of what I should do next. All of a sudden I feel an excruciating pain in my left shoulder. I scream out in pain and clutch my shoulder. I feel something warm and wet slowly spread across my hand. Dazed, I look at my hand, and I see deep red blood. Once again I feel a knife pressed against me, this time on my chest.

"If you do anything, I'll kill you."

I listen and decide to do what he says.

As we get in the house, I look over the abandoned street and feel a few drops of rain fall on my face, mingling with my tears.

The house is a mess. The floor is strewn with rubbish and dust flows freely around the rooms.

"Get in here."

He pushes me roughly into a room and I collapse upon a sofa. I feel tired and dizzy due to the loss of blood. Loose springs rip at my clothes and cut my arms and face. The pain in my arm is intense as I try to sit up, but I try to ignore it and keep focused.

The man is sitting there, staring at the floor uneasily. He can't even look at me now. I'm getting really scared now. What is he going to do to me?

"Empty your pockets," He orders.

I do what he says and remove my mobile and my purse from my pockets. Blood is now staining my jeans. I know that this cut is serious

I hand him the items and stare at a rat that's gnawing at a discarded cereal box. What is he going to do now?

My vision is starting to get blurry. I begin to close my eyes when the man finally speaks.

"Leave."

I look at him, hopeful and confused. Is he letting me go?

"Go. Get lost, and if you tell the police about this, you're dead! ... GO!"

I try to stand up quickly but my I fall back down. I stand up again, slowly this time. I sway unsteadily on my feet and trail towards the front door. I can feel the man's eyes piercing into my back.

Once I reach the front door, I run for it, as fast as I can, but I can only run for a few seconds before I collapse. My blood spreads across the pavement. I turn on my back and look up at the sky, rain covering my face, washing my blood into the gutter, and I thank God that the man let me go.

I smile slightly, as the rain stops. I see the sun beginning to peak though the clouds. A small bubble of hope rises inside of me. Then, complete darkness.

Rachel Concannon

Mirror

If I knew what was going to day happen that day, I would never have got out of bed. Not that I had a choice. The annoying, repetitive screeches of the alarm clock woke us both up at half past eight. He told me to "Get up, and get ready" without even a "Good morning". Not that it was going to be a good morning. A loud, exasperated yawn leapt out of my mouth as I clambered down the stairs. As I munched and chewed on the soggy piece of toast that was my breakfast, I could feel the anger welling up inside of him. Why? I don't know. I probably wasn't eating fast enough. I ate the rest of the toast quickly to avoid being shouted at. Then he spoke, "Go and have a shave. We've got to be out of here by ten." I trudged back up the stairs. Would he ever leave me alone and let me live my own life? I didn't try and argue or talk back to him. He had a very short temper. The only time that he couldn't boss me about was when I was at work. I was free of him then. That was the only time that I was in control of my life.

I went upstairs, and, as he ordered, I had a shave. After that he insisted I brushed my teeth because he thought my breath stank. So, I brushed them until they were spotless, and, as the thick bristles of the brush bashed around in my mouth, I silently cursed him. All this time I could see him in the mirror. He never took his eyes off me. His black pupils were concentrated on me, controlling me. He had me in his own personal prison.

We left the flat at 10 o'clock exactly. "To earn a little money," as he had told me. He had shown it to me before we left. It was sleek and shiny. Silver in colour. It was quite small; small enough to fit inside a pocket. He had started to go into detail, and tell me its name, but I had told him not to bother. A gun was a gun. And stealing was wrong. He put the gun in my pocket because I looked less suspicious.

His target was a bank on the other side of town. We would arrive there by bus, and leave there on foot. That way we could dispose of our outer garments and blend in to the huge mass of people going shopping, and allow them to swallow us up. He had definitely planned this carefully. We briskly walked the five minute stretch to the bus stop. It was a small, empty shelter with small, uncomfortable seats. We sat down and waited for the bus.

It was a crisp December morning. Mist hung in the air and clouds circled above like birds of prey. Were we their victims? The sky was a deep grey and the air was deathly cold. It slapped and stung my face, leaving raw, red marks. Every time I exhaled, my breath erupted from my lips as a visible cloud, swirling and twisting in the air before turning invisible a few feet in front of my eyes.

It arrived within a couple of minutes. It was a modern piece of machinery: ugly and dull. Chewing gum was stuck to the window, while crumbs, empty crisp packets and scrunched up tickets covered the floor. We cautiously boarded the bus. As he showed the driver our bus pass, I scanned the vehicle for any people. The bus driver himself looked completely harmless and friendly. He was middle aged, quite short, and spoke in a Scottish accent. He had a thin moustache that looked like it had been glued to his upper lip, and a lump of reddish brown hair was arranged like grass on top of his head.

In the middle of the bus, leaning his head against the window, sat a young college student. He looked to be no older than seventeen. His hair was as black as tar, and was glistening with sticky gel. He wore glasses, and, behind the clear lenses, his dark brown eyes stared vacantly into space. He was listening to music, and was unaware that he was breathing quite heavily.

Two seats in front of him was an old woman, at least in her seventies. She had a bored look on her face, and large glasses that magnified her beady eyes. She had several shopping bags and had presumably just been shopping.

On the back row, there was a rough looking man. He looked to be in his mid-thirties, and dangerous. He was quite tall and well built with a huge beer belly. Not one hair could be seen on his smooth scalp, and the light from outside reflected off his head and created a shimmering mirage of blinding light. And as for his face – a broken nose told the story of a violent man, who had been in his fair share of pub fights and didn't quite know how to control his temper. He looked quite tired, and probably had a hangover. His arms, his hand, and his neck were all covered with tattoos. The filthy scars curled around on his shin and writhed in agony in the form of dragons and other shapes.

The student, the old lady, and the skinhead occupied the right side of the bus, while on the left side sat a single man. He was about thirty with thin, black hair, which was a mess. It sat like a scraggly ball of string on top of his head. His weather-beaten face was covered in stubble. He sat there, slouched in his chair with a dreary look of boredom and weariness on his face. The only part of him that seemed to be alert was his eyes darting from here to there. They were large, black, radars, scanning the surroundings for danger. He wore a large, dirt-brown coat which fell to his knee height.

I heard a mumbled "Move along". I turned to see the driver looking at something behind us. We shuffled along the bus, and sat down behind the student, and opposite the man in the large coat.

No one else entered through the sliding doors, and they squeezed shut, blocking out the sound of the howling wind and the bustling of the crowd. Everything went silent. Very slowly the bus rolled away from the stop and started its journey, as we started ours. The world sped past the window. If I had looked out of the window, I would have seen many buildings: the bank, the building where I work, even the prison. However, I wasn't concentrating on the scenery. I was checking the bus for any change in the moods of the passengers. I could only see the back of the old lady's head, but the student hadn't moved. He was still glued to the window by his hair, and his music could be heard as a quiet fuzz of distortion. The escaping sound of music was very quiet, but loud enough to be the loudest sound on the bus. As for the skinhead, he was fumbling around in his jeans pocket for something. He found what he was looking for, smiled and withdrew his hand from his pocket with something in his grip. The sun glinted off it and it was so shiny, it was enticing. He held it momentarily, and then put it back into his pocket. He was more alert now. The man in the brown coat had also become alert too. His eyes had widened, and he had lost his slouch and was now sitting perfectly straight. The tension in the air that had been unnoticeable for so long, suddenly grew rapidly. Everyone was aware of each other; even the old lady at the front shuffled uncomfortably in her seat. Everyone except for the student. He sat there in a world of his own. He had become more and more relaxed. We could sense danger. I shifted uncontrollably, and he began to become restless and rigid.

Most of the journey was a blur, just like the scenery from the window view. I sat there wondering what was going to happen. I was nervous. He had reassured me not to be, but I was still nervous. I can't remember how long we were travelling for. It must have been about ten minutes before it happened.

I suddenly had this curious urge to see what was inside the skinhead's pocket. I slowly rotated my head around to look at him. If he caught me looking at him now, he would probably kill me. He was deep in concentration, looking out of the window. I looked at his jean pocket. Curiosity got the better of me. I looked at him for one second too long, and he looked up and made eye contact with me. He gave me a glare that I would never forget. His eyes shot a glance at me that pierced my eyes and filled me with fear and embarrassment.

"What are you looking at?"

The words were said with anger and a slight raise of the voice. The sentence tumbled out of his mouth in an insulting way and left me rattled. I turned round, blushing. His voice was enough to make everyone on the bus look around except for the driver. The old lady looked round disapprovingly, the man in the brown coat turned to look at me with a look of warning on his face, and the student took his earphones out of his ears and sat up straight to gain a better perspective of the situation.

It took less than a minute for everyone to stop looking at us and to go back to what they were doing before. Except the student didn't start listening to his music again. Whether he was getting off the bus quite soon, or afraid to miss another piece of drama, I don't know. What I do know is that he was now waiting for something to happen. And it did happen...

We had become uncomfortable with the situation as the student was listening to us, but we spoke anyway.

"What did you do that for?"

"I didn't mean to. I didn't think he would catch me."

"But why?"

"I was curious."

"No. You were being stupid."

"I'm sorry."

"Shut up."

"I am. I'm really sorry."

"Shut up now. Be quiet."

"But..."

"Shut up now." "Wha..."

I stopped.

The student had heard everything. He swivelled his head round to look at us through the gap in the seats. At that moment the bus drove over a dip in the road, and I held my hand out to lean against the window for support. That was my mistake. I only just realized that the gun was in my pocket and as I looked down the silver object of evil beauty slipped slowly out of my pocket and onto the seat. The student's face turned from confused to terrified and he sat there looking at me. I gave him a look as if to say "don't move" but he couldn't take a hint. He screamed the words and the fear quaked in his voice:

"He's got a gun..."

I was petrified with fear. I wanted to kill the student. It wasn't even my choice to be here and yet here I was. But I couldn't kill him. I could never shoot someone in cold blood. We stood up. So did the skinhead. So did the man in the coat. He held up both of his hands in an innocent gesture and said in a calming tone, "Drop the gun and calm down". The student was now on his mobile, calling the police. I suddenly realized that I had the gun in my right hand. I found out we were standing in the aisle. How we got there I don't know. We must have stumbled out there subconsciously. The student was to the left of us while the man in the coat stood to our right, hands in the air. My whole body was shaking uncontrollably. I could now see the skinhead reaching into his pocket and pull something out. A flick-knife. He started his lumbering journey towards me, his eyes filled with pure loathing. He must be either crazy or drunk. But he didn't look crazy, and how can anyone be drunk at half past ten in the morning? Drugs? Maybe. Or perhaps he was just looking for a fight. Whatever it was, my thinking didn't make him slower as he advanced on me. He was getting closer. A thin trickle of sweat departed from my forehead, trickled down my nose, dropped onto my parched lips. I could taste the drop of salt lying there on my lower lip, and it slowly began to move across my mouth as my trembling continued. It continued to torture me and forced me to salivate. All I had to do was wipe it away on my sleeve but my fear prevented me from doing so. The skinhead was now moving towards me, knife in hand, with frightening speed. He was ready to stab. Whether he meant to kill, I would never know.

I remembered that I still had the gun in my hand. It was the only thing stopping him from reaching me. Either I killed him or he killed me. Fear wanted me to fire, but my conscience stopped me from doing so. I had two choices: to die, or to go to jail. I raised the gun, and as a did, I knew I only had one choice. He was still approaching and I was still trembling. It took both my hands to steady the gun, and even then, my hands were still shaking tremendously while he kept coming. He was five metres away when my conscience gave in and fear took over. It happened in a blur. I pulled the trigger, and emptied the contents of the gun into him. Luckily for him, I couldn't aim properly and missed with most of my shots, but the few that did hit him, made their mark. The first bullet hit him in his right shoulder. The right side of his body was flown back and a spray of deep red blood leaped into the air behind him. The shot forced him to drop the knife, and it fell to the floor with a clatter. Why I kept shooting, I don't know. The second bullet missed his ear by an inch and completed its journey by smashing into the back window and sending shattered glass everywhere. The third bullet hit him with an unbelievable force in his chest, sending him sprawling left, arms flailing in the air. A gush of blood squirted out of the wound, and droplets of blood detached themselves from his mouth and were sent rocketing to the floor. The forth bullet slammed into a chair on the back row sending dust circling into the air like the clouds earlier that morning. The fifth hit the roof making a deafening clang. The sixth, final, and fatal bullet left the gun at a blistering speed, and embedded itself in his heart. He stuttered and then fell backwards, his eyes glistening. I slowly took a couple of cautious steps forwards and looked at the corpse I had created. His legs had crumpled under him and his arms were stretched wide reaching away from him. His t-shirt, once white, was now stained red, and his face was a bloody mess. His chin was bathed in blood and a pool of red was forming under his torso. We ran. The last thing I remember seeing on the bus was the student's innocent face staring at me. The doors were open, don't ask me why. We ran out and the gun fell from my limp hand. I remember running for less than twenty seconds before they caught us. I wondered how they knew where I was, then I realized the student probably gave them the location. I remember the sound of the sirens, and the taste of gravel and then everything went black.

The next month was a blur. I couldn't remember anything. We were both taken to the police station, to court, everywhere. I remember nothing. I want to remember nothing. I had killed a man. I had no choice. I had told them that, but nobody believed me. I shouted at them telling them I was innocent, but no one listened. Had I actually shot someone in cold blood, or was it self defence? I didn't even know what to think.

The next thing I remember, I was sitting in a cell. The whining wind whistled through the cracks in the stone, and the rain angrily lashed down on the prison. I was cold, I was hungry, and I was scared. It was a one man cell, yet we had still been put in here. We had one bed and one meal. It wasn't fair. The wind from the outside echoed off the blank walls making a horrific wailing sound that was pain to the ears.

The guard came with the dinner. He was a tall man who looked like he had forgotten why he wanted to work in a prison in the first place. His menacing uniform separated him from the rest of the prisoners. He ungratefully pushed the tray of food through the hole in the door. I received it with gratitude, and wolfed down the stone-cold stew. I licked the spoon until every morsel was gone and it was gleaming. It had become a mirror. I held it up to the light and looked into it, and he stared back at me.

Conor FitzPatrick

Ripper Rekindled

Monday 9.30 am

My fumbling fingers scratched at the newspaper. Beads of nerves, excitement and anticipation dripped down my cheeks, imitating tears of remorse that were nonexistent.

"Ripper Rekindled" the blotched, creased paper read, screaming at me success and joy.

See, I was the person who could make a difference and change the world; I wasn't as mad as people liked to think. My path was laid out for me many years ago; my destiny unchangeable and blessed.

I could feel my eyes glistening as I scanned the page; my body shook with triumph, my mission was finally recognized and no longer ignored. My hero was receiving the recognition he deserved and I was being compared to him, an achievement beyond my dreams.

The woman hadn't felt it. She was merely an instrument, a belonging at my disposal. I remember stirring the tea, her lined, creased face stretching into a smile and as I reined the blows on her, I watched the light leave her eyes and her face show only surprise.

I wasn't a medical student for no reason. My expertise was widely acknowledged and I used to be considered one of the best in my occupation.

She was unrecognisable when I disposed of her and although I was proud of what I was and what I had become, I didn't feel the necessity to expose myself to the outside world at this moment in time.

Monday 9.46 am

I looked out of the window, the sky a ghastly grey. I tugged at my beard, my forehead creased in concentration. 10 murders in a 15 mile radius was more then a coincidence in my opinion. It was my job to catch who was responsible.

The last attack was particularly brutal; an elderly woman murdered and disposed of as a pile of meat rather then a human. My stomach churned with anxiety and determination and my mission was undoubtedly clear.

My desire to catch those responsible was overwhelming and I knew if I didn't, the results may be unforgivable.

I stared into the mirror and all I saw back was a mop of thinning grey hair with a neatly trimmed beard to match. A pair of eyes, dark and resolute. My expression determined and final, I could do this.

Tuesday 7.16 am

The plan had formed in my mind. It was cunning, clever and unimaginable. My mind even amazed me sometimes. It was going to be difficult; there was no doubt about that.

I had my outfit ready, ironed and prepared. I felt as if I was created for this sole purpose. I was unique in my aim – I was invincible. My life's path glittering before me, beckoning me forward.

The tube was due in 6 minutes. I felt like any other commuter travelling to do their job, except mine was taking me to new places today. It was crammed. People smiled at me. If they knew who they were looking at their faces would show respect and reverence.

Tuesday 9.48 am

A pattern was emerging. If my calculations were correct then the killer would strike any time soon. Time was running out. Fast. I decided to travel to London. I had a rough idea of where the next attack would be.

10.51 am Tuesday

I stared at the sign above me, 'Madame Tussauds.' I had been many times before, but this was different. Before I had been a spectator, now I was a character for people to gawk at and marvel at how realistic I was.

I stationed myself perfectly; put the place-card by my feet.

My first audience soon appeared. "Jack the Ripper" they read, their eyes like saucers. Ha! If only you knew, I laughed; my plan was working to perfection.

Tuesday 1.53 pm

I hadn't seen anything so far. I received a call from the station, "can you go Madame Tussauds, they have an unusually large amount of visitors and need extra security?" It was useless to protest even if somebody's life was on the line. I trudged reluctantly over, my mind whirring with thoughts of the killer. He was an insane genius, who knows what he would do next?

I was starting to get bored and my mind was elsewhere. I couldn't rest until I found the murderer.

Suddenly, my mind was taken over by curiosity rather then concern. A new waxwork had been erected and he was unbelievably realistic. "Jack the Ripper" the card read. My eyes flickered to the other side of the hallway. There was the old waxwork of Jack the Ripper. How odd, I thought. Then thoughts of suspicion clouded my mind.

Tuesday 2.06 pm

My heart was racing, I had seen his face many times, appealing for people with information to come forward, for me to hand myself in; what was I to do? I saw his eyes caressing me, they were mingled with suspicion and accusation.

My time has come I thought. I had to leave; maybe I should run for it? Before I really thought about what I was doing, or what consequences my actions may provoke, my legs broke into a run on impulse.

Tuesday 2.21 pm

He must have seen the realisation in my eyes, the glitter and the happiness. He began to run, lunging at people with the blade in his podgy hand. I ran as I had never run before in my life, as if my life, not his, depended on it.

Then to my amazement he tripped, his agile body falling into the arms of the real waxwork who he had longed to be so desperately. My whole body shook as the knife of the real waxwork pierced his skin with precision and edge. He lay lifeless on the floor, blood seeping silently from within him. Killed by his desire and obsession.

Nicole Glennon

Diary

Sunday 25th June.

I don't want to, I can't. I hate school, Mum and Dad know but they say that they can't do anything about it. They hate me, all of the kids at school, they hate me, they pick on me, they laugh at me, they hit me and punch and kick me. They call me names, they try to do everything that they can to try and make me crack. But I won't, I won't fall and crumble. I won't fall into their hands that easily, I'll show them that I'm not stupid, I'm not thick, I know what they're trying to do, but I won't fall, I'm strong. Not weak, I won't let them get away with this, I'll show them.

Annie, how could I forget about her? She's beautiful. No, she is more than beautiful, her shining blue eyes, her warm gentle smile, she is the only person who keeps me going through all of the trouble that I am going through, at least she understands.

But school, why does it even exist? Why can't there be a place where me and Annie could run away together and live together forever, no school, no more bullying, no more hatred, just me and Annie in our own little world. That would be perfect. But it could never happen.

She has a nice, caring family who all love her dearly, who praise her and give her all of the confidence that she needs to get on with her life. My family don't love me, sometimes I get the feeling that I don't even belong to them, that I'm just some random object that has been stuck to their shoes and won't come away. Mum seems like the only person who actually cares. She tells me that everything will work out one day and that I will not need to think about all of those horrible people who hate me. But although she cares, it seems most likely that she doesn't really understand, not properly.

I don't think that anybody can understand how I feel, what I am really going through. Not even Annie, no matter how much I try to believe her and what she tells me, it doesn't seem real, it's like I'm stuck down in the deepest, darkest pits of hell, and there Annie is, up in heaven having the time of her life. If there were such things as guardian angels then Annie would undoubtedly be mine. And I know that if there really is a devil then it would be Matthew Rice.

He is the leader of them, the boys who like to beat the hell out of me. Do they do it for fun or do they do it for them, to try and make themselves look big, tough and strong? If I had my way then I'd, I'd... Oh, I don't know what I would do, so what's the point? I feel as if I can't take it any more, I can't survive one day without not being hit, punched, kicked, tormented, told that I'm an idiot and I don't belong here. How many times does someone have to put up with something they hate? Sometimes not very long at all, sometimes they have to stand back and wait until it's stopped. But it is not like that for me.

Every day I watch it happen to me, I feel it happen to me. Mum has gone into school umpteen times, but the same thing happens every time.

Mum goes in and complains, the four boys get told off and are given a warning, Mum leaves, thinking that everything is fine, the boys come back, find me, and start to beat the hell out of me again.

IT NEVER STOPS !!!

Monday 26th June

It was hell at school today, why is it always me, why am I always the target, why, why, why?! They hate me. Why? They think I'm stupid. A fat, ugly, nobody. Why in all the earth does it have to be me?! Matthew Rice. Why him? Anybody else would be bad enough, but him, the torment of all torment, the bully of all bullies, what is wrong with him? Or what is wrong with me?

Every morning I look in the mirror and what do I see? A blob, a big, huge, greasy spotty, fat and ugly blob. Voices start to swim around in my head. Watch you don't break the mirror John, or seven year's of bad luck could be heading your way if you keep looking in that mirror for too long.

Please leave me alone, I feel like screaming, what is so wrong with me, why am I the easy target, the one who seems like he can't stand up for himself?

Annie doesn't think like that though, she would never think about me like that, not ever, she loves me, or at least I think she does. But what if she doesn't love me – or even like me! Oh God! What if it turns out that she doesn't like me and that she was really working undercover for Matthew Rice and his friends. But I've told her all of my secrets, that I would never tell anybody, all of the times that I have been through which were thoroughly embarrassing. What if she is working undercover, what if she tells them, what will I do? Oh my God!

But think wisely John, Annie would never do that, she's a caring girl who promised me in Florida that she would always be here to help me and comfort me.

But what if she lied to me? What if she had her fingers crossed behind her back when she made that promise, what if it was all part of her undercover act?

Stop it John, you're just being stupid, Annie isn't like that. She loves you. Remember, she cares about you, she wants to help you through all of the problems that you are having. She is your friend, don't think otherwise. Besides, it's not like she wanted to know everything about you, she said that she wanted to be your friend.

Those words, she wanted to be your friend. Why are those words now stuck in my head? Oh God, that one word – wanted. What if she doesn't really want to be my friend!

OK John, this is just some crazy and bizarre moment that you've been having. None of this is for real. What are you thinking of? Annie is not like this, you're crazy John, crazy I tell you.

Maybe I am crazy, maybe I am losing my mind, perhaps I'm just some crazy child, mental even, but is it my fault?

NO!

It's those stupid boys at school. They have driven me to it.

NO!

They haven't.

Not yet.

Tuesday 27th June

They've done it again, I knew that they would. But it's not the same as usual. No, it's worse. I was right, they have and I knew that they would.

It's Annie. She's been acting strange, no – weird.

They've taken her, I know they have, she wasn't at school today, but all of her friends knew where she was.

She is an undercover spy, and she is working for them. They've taken her,

110

I'm positive, but where they have taken her, I don't know.

An undercover spy, where would she have been sent? Oh no. What if she's here in the house.

I locked the door when I came in.

What if she climbed through a window?

All of the windows in the house are shut.

The back door?

I locked it.

Under the bed?

OK then John, your imagination has totally gone wild, and mad. There is no possible way that Annie could be hiding under your bed.

But what if she followed me into the house?

John, she didn't follow you into the house, you would have known she was there. How would I have known that she was there?

You would have heard her or most likely seen her.

OK. Maybe I am going crazy, maybe I am losing my mind, and what if there is something really wrong with me. I can't tell anyone, not Mum no way could I tell stress hound (Dad), he would say that I was really mad and he'd most likely start having a good old moan at me. I especially can't tell Annie, what if she is lurking in the room somewhere right now? What if she can read my thoughts? What if she can somehow see what I am writing?

I have to stop writing but I can't. I can't help thinking that tomorrow my whole life may come crashing down on me and it would all have been because of Annie.

John, you can't he seriously thinking that Annie is an undercover spy who is more than willing to work for Matthew Rice and the other boys because I don't know how many times you have reminded yourself.

ANNIE IS NOT LIKE THAT!!!

What was that?

It must have been Annie.

No John, it's not Annie.

How am I supposed to know that for sure?

I'm really sure that I just heard the door open.

I locked the door.

Thankfully it was only Mum, she had got back home from work early.

Then, the phone rang, not the house phone, my mobile.

Who was it?

What did they want?

I looked at the number on the screen.

It was Annie.

Wednesday 28th June

Annie was back. Where had she been? What had she been doing? Could she have been ill? Could she have been following me?

I didn't want to talk to her. I couldn't just tell her about all of the crazy thoughts that I had had about her being an undercover spy for the bullies.

Her eyes were shining brighter than ever, her smile was warmer than ever too. She looked happy.

She was happy.

At lunchtime she came over to me and asked me why I hadn't answered her call last night.

I couldn't look her in the eye.

She asked me again. Her voice was so soft.

I couldn't answer her.

I ran. I kept on running, I couldn't seem to stop. I needed to run faster than I had ever run before.

It happened again.

I stopped in the far corner of the playground to try and regain my breath.

They were there, waiting for me. They must have followed me there themselves. I then realized that I had been wrong about Annie all along. She was a caring, kind girl who was trying to help me sort out my problems.

My mind was taken away from the four boys standing around me as I reminded myself that I had been wrong.

Then it happened.

A blow in the stomach. A kick in the shin. A slap round the face. After they had all run away, I was left alone in the corner, doubled over and with a bleeding nose too. Couldn't move, it hurt so much.

A playtime assistant finally saw me kneeling on the floor, still doubled up in pain. She tried to move me but I couldn't. It was too painful.

When I got home I switched on my mobile and that was when I saw them. Three text messages.

One from Matthew.

One from one of the other boys.

One from Annie.

I read the one from Matthew and to my greatest surprise, it wasn't threatening. It was an apology. I read it through over and over again. I had to delete it. It was one of their traps. To try and make me forgive them and then they would start the bullying all over again.

The second message was from Luke, one of the other boys who was part of the gang. It was not the same kind of message that Matthew had sent me. In fact it was the exact opposite. A threatening message that was telling me that if I did tell on them again then I would really be for it.

The third and final message was from Annie. I was surprised by this message too. She said that she had seen what had happened to me at lunchtime and that she hoped that I had been found by the playtime assistant because she was the one who had sent her. I replied to her message saying how grateful I was. She didn't reply.

Thursday 29th June

I have made my mind up.

I'm not going to put up with this any more.

I'm not going to let them get to me.

They won't pick on me any more.

They won't call me names.

They won't hit me, kick or punch me.

They won't annoy me.

But how do I tell Mum and Dad?

Should I or shouldn't I?

I couldn't tell Annie. That was for sure. Her heart was so tender, I couldn't let it be broken over something like this. It would almost rip her in half We loved each other.

And there was something so special about Annie that I couldn't let her know what I was going to do.

And Mum and Dad, even though they didn't show it most of the time, I knew that deep down inside they loved me really.

Or do they?

Katrina McNair

Dramatic Monologues

I'm getting too old for this - Batman

Some people think I'm mad, crazy, cuckoo
That I've got a screw - and a few bolts - loose.
Others think I'm an almighty hero
Saving the city, defending the innocent,
And all that jazz... I'm neither.
I'm human - an ordinary nothing-special human
I just break more bones, that's all.
It all started - the whole 'Batman' gig
Because of a single person
And the death of two others, I suppose.
'Heartless!' I hear you cry
Speaking as if my parents meant nothing
To me at all.
But that's just it, I'm the Dark Knight
Courageous but emotionless
Feared by all - even those
I risk my life to protect.
Even sometimes by my family...
No! Not mine, never mine!
Bruce's - Bruce Wayne, that is -
The happy-go-lucky billionaire
The one with an adoptive son
And a caring father-figure.
A completely separate person,
Or another side of the same coin.
But I'm really not who others think I am.
I am not heatless - even though
It's dangerous to get emotionally attached.
I am not fearless - but I would
Risk everything for those I love.
I am brave; I am weak
I am Bruce; I am Batman
I am me...
And I think I'm too old for this charade...

Samantha Smith

Bliss

I am passion, I am love, I am relief.
I am the silver lining, the pearl in the field,
a treasure lost at sea, the dreams and hopes,
I glorify the land and spread flourishing happiness.

When a child is born, I am there,
When a couple are wedded, I am there,
When the phoenix cries and the poor are enriched, I am there,
I am the aura, the Northern Lights, the Golden Gates.

I am outstretched arms, welcoming warmth,
the calming ripple of the river across the pebbles,
the serene cascades of water over a cavern,
I am the spirit of the sky, the air and the clouds.

When the stars twinkle, the magnificence of nebulas,
the sound of a castrata, the calling of an angel,
I rescue those in danger, I comfort those in need,
I am bliss.

Thomas Newman

Anger

I am slits and knives, blades and épées,
slices of corrugated iron, smouldering sulphur,
I am diesel-fuelled fire, unstoppable and raging,
I am a child that has been given the wrong toy car for
their birthday.

I am the firing guns of soldiers, the bleeding of their wounds,
the tension, the gripping fists and the sinews clenching.
I am relentless retaliation and heavy breathing,
I am glorious red like the piercing crimson strikes of lightning.

I am the swelling, the sickness, the fury and the adrenalin,
I am the irrational actions of drunken adolescents at a party.
I am flaring, ostentatious, outrageous,
I cross the line, I push the boundaries.

I emanate fire from nothing,
I evade my flare from calming down,
I am sharp shards of metal, ripping the soul to shreds,
I am anger.

Thomas Newman

Bliss

I am Bliss. I am the one
who ensnares your senses
and releases your inner child.

I am Bliss, I chuckle happily
while I tickle you in the right spot.
and you enjoy it. It releases your soul.

I am Bliss. I glide in your mind,
yellow robes floating behind me
waking your imagination.

Yet sometimes you kill me
with your filthy anger and outrageous thoughts.
I struggle to calm you down.
I am a question of willpower
as well as imagination.

Chloe Crichton

Anger has feeling

I'm burning inside my dark padded cell,
Crouching... my face indescribable.
I am the one that shines RED in the pit of your gut.
I am anger, I am angry.
I am the one you fear.

I jump up, pace this dungeon
That cuts me off from civilized man.
Longing to be released, longing to lash out
At that waste of skin and bone who made me like this.
I am anger.

I roar, hiss with frustration,
My red robe billowing behind.
The passion to kill amazingly intense.
No weapons... Just my bare hands.
I am anger.

Must be released; I'm growing more aggravated.
Towering high on the edge of my sanity.
Please release me. I don't want to exist any more.
I am anger.

Chloe Crichton

Save me – Robin

Look at the everyday,
Where your heart and future lies.
Can you see past the laughter?
Can you hear all the cries?
They're normal people in normal days
But I can see the sorrow
So clearly written on their faces
Because they fear the tomorrow.
When again I must be their hero.
They who work and toil will fall
And when they reach rock-bottom
I must save them all.
Physically, I may weaken,
But I'll never stop
I will do everything to keep them alive
People of this earth
Heed my world now
Even if it kills me I'll make you survive...
For the saviour can never be saved...

Samantha Smith

War

A Soldier's Tale

The land around was a bloody mess. Bodies lay blood stricken against the remains of houses. The smell of the rotting wounds hung in the air like a lingering mid-morning fog. For the first time in many days my ears heard nothing. No gun fire. No dropping of shells. No eerry cries of wounded young men horrifically dying on the battlefield. The sky was silent. Too silent The sun beamed down onto my face as I cleared the sweat off my brow.

I had a nasty headache due to a mixture of my helmet digging in to my temples, and having four hours sleep in the last three nights. But all the lads were in the same position as me so I could not complain. Private Peters and Private Johnson had been positioned at the top of a bell tower, a good thirty feet higher than any other building in the surrounding area. Private Johnson was the best sniper the entire English army had, well in my opinion anyway, so he was happy being positioned high above any oncoming Germans. As for Peters, he was the most unruly character of us all and the lieutenant wanted him up high were he could not get himself blown to pieces!

I was positioned about twenty feet from the foot of the bell tower, just waiting for the Germans to fall into our trap. We didn't have many men but we all knew our jobs, and what was at stake if we did not carry them out with the utmost composure. Other than Peters, Johnson and me, there was Privates Livingston, Wilson, Roberts and Parker stationed fifty feet behind me along the street. The street was narrow and the rubble from blown up houses created a bottle neck pathway for a few hundred feet. Our plan was to lure the Germans along this street and ambush them. But with limited men and ammo, it was going to have to be pulled off with absolute precision and perfection.

I had made some makeshift 'Sticky Bombs' out of the available resources and some TNT, which we were using to blow up the bridge and it was the only form of ammunition we had in abundance. Once we had ambushed and hopefully annihilated the Germans, we would retreat back down the street and blow up the bridge there. It was a crucial bridge for the Germans so if we were successful in destroying it, we would be hitting the Germans where it hurt. We had some idea, but we were not certain, of what we were going to be up against. Private Parker had somehow manage to acquire a

129

Panzershriek, maybe with only eight shells, but it was enough to take out a few tanks. My sticky bombs could disarm a few more tanks.

We had two men in the bell tower, six men behind walls of sandbags on either side of the road, me and the lieutenant slightly further up the street and Privates Livingston, Wilson, Roberts and Parker bringing up the rear. Everyone was equipped with a rifle and a couple of grenades and other than a few mines in the middle of the road, that's all we had. So it was just a waiting game.

When we heard the Germans coming at the top of the road, a couple of soldiers would go and show themselves then quickly run back into position and hope the Germans had taken the bait. Private Roberts, a man I had grown increasingly fond of, began to tell me of his eldest brother Jack as we were sitting in the blistering heat of the midday sun. It was very moving because Roberts had just been told of how his brother died in action. I could closely relate to him after seeing dozens of my own men die before my very eyes. The rest of the lads had salvaged an old gramophone and were playing some German song that Private Wilson was translating. He was the only foreign-speaking person among us and, as far as I could see, this was his only skill. He hadn't even handled a rifle before last week.

It was a good couple of hours before I heard the low, distant droning of the German tanks over the buzz of the gramophone. My ears pricked up as I slung my rifle over my shoulder. I shouted to the other lads to get into position and I followed the lieutenant to mine as the vast amounts of adrenaline started to pump around my body. You could almost smell the fear among us all as the sound of the tanks grew increasingly audible. I made a last check that my rifle was loaded and my spare ammo was to hand. We were all set and I made sure the boys knew exactly what they were doing with my sticky bombs.

Privates Parker and Roberts were sent to go and lure the Germans. They ran to the end of the street where there was a T-junction where the Germans were going to be passing. The two men made themselves visible to the oncoming troops by climbing high onto what looked like the remains of a church. They both fired a few rounds in the Germans direction then scattered back down the street into their prearranged positions. The grinding of the tanks grew louder still. Johnson was signalling down to me from the top of the bell tower. There were 6 tanks and about fifty infantry. The first tank slowly became visible at the top of the street. I crouched behind a pile of sandbags. To my surprise it didn't turn down towards us.

Then another drove past and didn't fall into our trap. We were just about to make a plan B when the third of the six tanks stopped at the top of the street, slowly angled itself towards us, and proceeded on its long-winded trek. The plan had worked. We had lured them into our trap.

The tank was slow on its approach, and I could see troops spilling out from behind it. We had to time our attack cleverly. I picked my man, rested my rifle on a sandbag and took aim. We had to wait for the unsuspecting troops to draw in closer. Wait for it. Wait for it. Fire! The lieutenant gave the order. I managed to keep my nerve, pull back my quivering forefinger and shoot down my man. In actual fact, it was a quite spectacular shot. Right on the forehead. From then on, the shots came flying from all angles. They still hadn't realized what had hit them when our two men opened fire from the top of the bell tower.

But our major priority at the time was to disarm those tanks before our two men in the bell tower came under siege. They wouldn't have a hope in hell if one of those German tanks had a clear shot at them. I pulled back my rifle and ducked below the sandbags with my back wedged against them. The first tank was grinding its way through the street. Their terrified troops were holding back and using the tanks for cover. As the first tank began to make its way past me, I rolled onto my side, crawled over to the side of the tank, pulled the pin off one of my bombs and planted it on the tracks of the tank. Private Wilson did this consecutively to the second tank as all of the surrounding men dived to the side of the road to find what cover they could from the bombs. The blasts were not very big but were big enough to stop the tanks in their tracks and they were successful in doing so. After the first two tanks, two men ran out from the opposite side of the road and planted bombs on the last two tanks. They too were successful.

I picked up my rifle once again and rested it on the now crippled wall of sandbags as some dazed and confused Germans began to emerge from the bullet-pierced tanks. All of our men started to pick off each and every man as a few grenades were thrown from somewhere behind me. Private Parker was also firing shells out of his Panzershriek from behind me which were successfully destroying the tanks. A wash of machine gun fire struck the enemy from the bell tower like a torrential hail storm. Every gust of dusty wind made the hairs on my neck stand on end. All was going well until I heard a low buzzing noise in my ear. It was growing in intensity as I grew in anxiety. I looked up at the bell tower and Private Johnson signalled down to me. There was a loud scream from behind where I was standing.

131

I vaguely heard the words get down over the gunfire. A moment later the most harsh sound filled my ears as I felt the most excruciating pain in my right arm. Three German Messerschmidt's had flown over and showered our men with machine gun fire. Our ambush had been ambushed! I was hit and some of our men appeared to be worse off than I was. We couldn't wait for anyone as the lieutenant ordered us to retreat to the bridge.

My eyes flashed up to the bell tower and I just caught Private Johnson and Peters heads vanish from the window. Several men, including the lieutenant, were sprinting back along down the street towards the bridge where some explosives had been set. But there was nowhere near as many men as there should have been. I plucked up all my remaining energy and started to hobble back towards the bridge. By this time most of our remaining men were already on the far side of the bridge and that somehow included Private Peters and Johnson. I was still dragging myself along the side of the road down to the bridge where a machine gun had been set up and was firing back up the street. I managed to pull myself to the far side of the bridge and everyone took cover as the explosives were detonated.

We succeeded in destroying the bridge and the few remaining Germans that tried to run at us were shot down. Our mission objectives had been completed. The lieutenant gathered us all together and congratulated us all on our performance. But many young men had been killed and in particular two very dear and close friends of mine. The mood among us all was very solemn to say the least as we all pondered the losses of all of our great friends and whether or not our mission was actually worth the lives of so many.

Chris Barrett

Legionnaires

There were five of us. Four of them, and myself. Each one of them had taken a corner to guard. The formation they had lined up in reminded me of the formation they take when guarding a Caesar, each man would throw his body in front of anything that was used to attack their leader even if it meant they would meet their death. I however, was the opposite. To them I was the enemy. The man that had been ordered to death by their superior leader.

We had not travelled a great distance only three miles or so, we trampled over what was now Roman land. A black scar lay to the right of us. Only a few days before this had been a lively forest, full of life and movement. Now it lay in ruins. When the battle had taken place we had used fire to destroy our barbarian enemies. This had a devastating impact on the land and vegetation around. That day seemed an age ago. I was leading the Romans to battle that day as their general. I had the respect of thousands of men; most of whom would have happily laid down their life for me. And now, just a few days later, the Empire that I had been serving for almost three years had sentenced me to death.

The five horses that we were riding slowed as we reached the trees. Maybe it was the dense, silver mist that made them slow or maybe it was the sense of unease and death that was bought to my body when being around this area. The hairs stood up on the back of my neck and a shiver ran down my spine as I inhaled the thick putrid air that surrounded me. The wind picked up as we arrived as if to warn us that this was a place for the dead and those who lived and dared to enter were unwelcome. As far as the eye could see, bodies lay rotting, skeletons and carcasses lay in piles. These bones were all that was left of the five hundred brave men that had tried to stop our army. They had tried to protect their land, their livelihood, and their lives; unfortunately for them there were far too many us.

Given the order from one of the legionnaires the horses would stop. Two men would come no further. They would stay on the outskirts of the forest and wait with the horses for the job to be done. Then the four would leave. I was ordered down from my horse. My hands were bound tightly; I jumped off my horse with great difficulty. I quickly felt the tip of a sword at my neck. I froze. The sharp cold metal sent waves of fear and adrenaline through my body, I could feel my heart beating quickly in my chest, sweat trickled slowly down my back. In my left ear I heard a deep rough voice, the voice said only one word "Follow".

I was led into the forest. The sword still pressed into my neck started to draw blood as its razor sharp point pierced my skin. Small droplets of blood ran like rain drops onto the earth. The land, still parched from the fire, days earlier, welcomed the moisture from my body and absorbed the blood within fractions of seconds like a thirsty man takes a drink. The mist was hanging in a thick layer on the floor as well as in the air, its denseness covered the bodies that lay on the floor but occasionally, as the mist swirled and moved, the outlines of the bodies could be seen. They did not look old and rotten; fresh red blood was visible on some of the bodies glimmering and shining in the misty layer. The smell of decay lingered in the air and mould and algae was visible on some of the bodies, a sign that the dead had been there for some time. I was led into a clearing. It was not far from where we had dismounted our horses. If not for the mist, it would have been possible to see the horses and the two legionnaires standing waiting for the job to be done. The clearing was not very large, about three paces wide. There was thick moss on the floor; I felt it on my knees as I was pushed downwards. As I knelt I remember praying to God to watch over my wife and son. The two legionnaires stood over me. One in front, one behind. I looked down still praying to God to protect my wife and son. The legionnaire behind drew his sword. The sound made from the metal skimming the metal whistled into my ears and down my body like a high pitched screaming noise. I looked round to find him now standing to the side of me. "At least give me a clean death!" I said. He understood exactly what I meant and took a few paces around my body so my back was facing him. The tip of his sword lay on my neck again. I winced with pain as he touched the cut previously made from his sword. He drew up! This was my chance! This is when I struck!

As he began to bring the sword down I arched up bringing my head into his chin. Before he could react I pulled the sword from his hands span round and smashed the handle over the head of the other legionnaire. He groaned in pain and fell backwards. With the blade held firmly in my hands I turned round and forced the sword into the first legionnaires chest. Blood stained the floor as it ran from his mouth and chest. He fell to his knees swayed in mid air then toppled backwards. Killing was not new to me and although I hate very much to take a life I knew that I would need to take more lives to ensure my safety. I turned and as I did, I threw the sword in the air and caught the handle. As I completed my turn, I swung my sword. I felt the blade smash across the face and helmet of the second legionnaire. The sound of metal hitting metal rang through the air and vibrated in my ears. My victim was killed instantly and fell face down onto the floor. A pool of his own blood formed around his head, the sight of my victim laying in his own blood made me feel sickened at what I had done. In the distance I heard a horse gallop. The other two legionnaires had heard the sword hitting their colleague's helmet and had come to see what was going on. I doubled off into the mist poised and ready to strike, ready to kill again.

In cover of a tall tree I hid for a few minutes leaving the legionnaires confused and baffled as to where I had gone. I was waiting for the right moment, waiting to strike! In the distance about twenty paces away I saw one of my enemies on their horse. He was looking around confused and scared. I could just about make out the expression on his face, the expression of fear was written on him, his nostrils were flared as if sniffing the sky for my scent; he was breathing heavily almost panting like a frightened dog. I could almost smell his fear in the air, and taste it on my lips. I looked down at the golden hilt of the sword I was carrying. Blood still stained the blade, red droplets of my murderous action dripped slowly onto the hard earth, mingling with the soil making it appear black. I grasped the hilt in my still bound hands and with all my might I lifted my sword high into the air, it sailed through the mist until it landed deep into the flesh of the legionnaire who was still sitting on the horse. His face appeared to be void of emotion, his eyes were wide open as if he were about to start a conversation with me. The blade struck and with an almighty thud he fell from his horse and was greeted by a deep black hole that took him to the afterlife.

There was now only one legionnaire left. The mist appeared to have lifted, I could see him clearly. I stepped out into the clearing that was meant to be the place where I would meet my Maker. I shouted "Legionnaire!" He turned on his horse and looked at me. I squatted with my sword behind my head ready to smash him from his horse when he charged. He looked upon my position as a challenge and began to charge. He charged at full pace anger in his face ready to avenge his colleagues that I had just slain. His deep blue cloak swayed in the air for what seemed like an eternity. Time seemed to stand still. I was still crouched waiting for the perfect time to launch my attack. Too soon and I was dead – too late and I was dead. His horse was only four paces away from me; it was then that I put my plan into action. I swiftly moved a few paces to my right and launched the metal blade into his chest as hard as I could. I felt a sharp pain on my left shoulder. His horse rode on, to my relief without its owner who lay motionless on the floor. I speared the blade of the sword into the ground. Angered that he had almost been too quick for me I slipped my fingers under my shoulder guard to find blood oozing out of a deep cut on my shoulder.

A sense of fear, guilt and relief washed over me like a wave.

Fear that my life had nearly been taken; guilt that I had taken so many lives and relief that I was alive.

Joe Moore

The Mogadishu Mile

My name is Jeff Collins. It was my seventeenth birthday when I joined the US army and by my nineteenth I had already seen more combat than many soldiers do in a lifetime. I was a US ranger based in Somalia, East Africa, a country torn apart by civil war between rival clans. Over 300,000 civilians died from starvation and warfare. Our job was to try and put an end to it. Mohamed Farrah Aidid was the most powerful of the warlords and controlled Mogadishu, the capital of Somalia; we were to take him apart general by general.

It was mid afternoon, October 3, 1993. This was our first mission; a simple one, four chalks of rangers were to secure a perimeter around the streets of the target building, whilst a team of Delta Force operators drop in to arrest the target generals. Should take no more than thirty minutes. The mission did not go so simply; they knew we were coming. It was an ambush.

The code name to signal the mission sounded through the barracks 'Irene, Irene' a frantic race to get ready began. The barracks were full, everyone buzzing with excitement and anxious to begin the mission. Little did they know that nineteen American lives were to be claimed and over 1000 Somalis. Everyone now fully equipped with weapons and armour began to climb into the Black Hawks. With all checks done and confirmation to go, the helicopters began to touch off the ground in synch like a group of pigeons startled by small child. I was on board one of the leading Black Hawks. I was sitting next to Private Jason Moore. He was my best friend. We had battled through all of the hardships that the army had thrown at us, basic training, jump school, ranger school, we had thrown ourselves out of planes and helicopters and now we were going to war together. If I knew anyone could get me through it, it would be him. Below us I could see the snaking path of the convoy. It threw up tall clouds of dust behind it as it made its way to the city; its role in all of this was to supply support and provide an escape for the ground troops after they had made their arrests.

Somalia was a poor, arid country that had felt the full effects and devastation of starvation and war. Our target building was in one of the last few remaining groups of large buildings that were fully intact. It was three stories tall and made with stone that had been whitewashed. It had windows but they were not covered by glass. The rest of the town was just blocks of irregular metal-roofed dwellings and dirty, unpaved streets.

137

Our helicopters reached the drop off points and began the insertion. We abseiled down into the middle of the street; it was impossible to see a thing, the choppers were blowing up the dust from the dry streets and making a smokescreen for us to land in. We had practised this and we all knew our roles: land, check the area, take cover and make a perimeter then just hold off the enemy until the convoy picked us up. We were like a well-oiled machine moving quickly and efficiently. I found myself a safe position lying behind some scraps of metal where I could pick off anyone armed who came my way. I had never actually shot a gun at anyone before. I had done it a thousand times in training but never at an actual person. The first few shots really affected me; it seemed so different when there was a live person receiving one of your bullets. This is something you could never be trained for. I just had to keep convincing myself that it was him or me. At that moment in time the fighting was not that intense; it was mainly the odd few people running at you or a technical would come flying around the corner. A technical is basically a car, usually a four by four with a .50-Cal gun on the back, simple but they cause a lot of trouble when you're trying to defend a position.

After ten minutes we received confirmation that the mission was a success and the captured enemy generals were ready to be evacuated. The men began to get restless and lose concentration as we waited for the convoy to arrive. "This battle isn't over yet. We don't know what the enemy has planned." With that said from captain Roberts the men settled again. Captain Roberts was in charge of our section in this operation. He was a tough, battle hardened man who everybody feared but respected. He had seen war before and we all felt he knew what he was doing and would be the person to get us through this.

"He's dead." These were the words that silenced the radios. The first fatal casualty of the operation had occurred. Everyone fell silent and took a minute. No friendly deaths were expected but I soon came to realize that would not be the last. "We've got large groups of militia heading towards your positions." The helicopters hovering above at 500 feet were advising us on the enemy positions, warning us what we were about to come up against. Soon enough, crowds of militia were swarming on our position. I was still in my same position behind some scrap metal. I began to hear shouting and screaming then hundreds of militia came marching around the corner. Men, women, and children, some clutching guns and firing in all directions; they were wary of our guns but edging in. I began to fire my M16 again trying only to hit the armed. "Where's the convoy ? We've got two men down," Captain Roberts screamed down the radio. Private Wolcott was lying motionless on the floor behind the building wall, he had been hit in the chest by a stray bullet. Private First Class Mark Good, the medic was arched over him trying to give CPR but it looked like it was to no avail. "Hang in there, come on hang in," he began to repeat. Captain Roberts walked over to them and placed his hand on Good's shoulder. "He's dead; you did all you could; now the other men need you." Good fell back against the wall and put his head in his hands, then after about three seconds he scrambled to his feet and picked up his rifle. The crowd soon became mainly militia and the women and children began to flee from sight.

"Get clear of the street we're coming in for a sweep." We all heard this over the radio, we fell back under the cover of the building. I sat behind a white structural pillar and clutched my gun. The sound of the helicopters rotors began to near. Machine gun fire opened up on the street then followed by a barrage of rockets that scattered down the road; the helicopters passed us so I poked my head out. The little birds kept firing and reduced the crowd to about half. "Get your head back in, you want to get yourself killed ?" Moore shouted through a thin gap in the wall. "We're coming back, stay clear." The machine gun fire started again and this time it was closer to us. Bullets began to smash against the pillar splintering the stone and sending shards in all directions.

The helicopters faded into the distance and the street was quiet. We began to move outside covering each other as we went "Everyone all right?" Captain shouted. "Yeah, Cap" the men replied.

"I just got word the convoy is en-route to our position" but before Captain Roberts could finish we could hear the sound of the engines. The Humvees and trucks came flying around the corner firing at the few militia that pursued them from the buildings and alleys. The convoy of four green Humvees and two big trucks came to a halt in front of us. The doors swung open and men poured out, assessing the street for enemy threats. Lieutenant Colonel Gary Harrell stepped out of the lead Humvees. He had a sense of calmness about him, he walked over to captain Roberts and began talking, you could tell what he said was bad and enraged Roberts. We gathered around Captain Roberts. "With the unexpected casualties there isn't much room left in the convoy. Four of us will have to run alongside. It's going to be about a fifteen minute journey. I'll be going, I need three more"

"I'll go captain" Sergeant Barrett stepped forward

"I'll go" Private Mark Good loaded a fresh magazine in to his M16 and went to stand near Barrett. Private Moore sat up I'll be your last man sir"

"I'm coming as well" I said to the Captain.

"Are you sure we really only need four people?"

"Yes, I couldn't leave you lot."

"Get ready we move in three minutes," Captain Roberts shouted to the men.

The convoy began to move. The five of us jogged alongside one of the trucks. The deafening cries of the injured men sounded from underneath the canvas sheets covering the truck. Moore looked over at me in horror, astounded by the noise of the crying men. We went for about three minutes with little resistance winding our way through the labyrinth of random, unmapped streets following the directions relayed to us from the helicopters. We came to a block in Mogadishu; it had towering buildings which engulfed the road. All of sudden the street erupted in a vicious fire fight. Small orange fire balls from the AK-47s lit the windows. The entire convoy engaged the enemy. The men in the Humvees gunner seats were frantically firing into every window arch, not giving time to see if it was occupied by enemy soldiers. I ducked behind the truck trying to use it as cover from the immense enemy fire. Captain Roberts ran up to an emplaced .50-Caliber that a Somali had just been shot from and began to gun down the men in the windows.

"They're leaving us, Captain they're leaving us," Moore yelled as the convoy began to accelerate.

"Enemy fire is too heavy we need to evac the wounded, regroup and come back in," Colonel Harrell radioed through to captain Roberts. "You'll have to go the rest on your own, good luck!"

The five of us grouped together and began to make our way through the back alleys of Mogadishu, heading north to the closest non-hostile territory. The alleys were still littered with enemy militia armed with AK-47s. Luckily the Somali were not the best shooters in the world and our chalk had been awarded for our marksmanship in training. We came to a corner and we did not check it properly. It resulted in a death.

140

It was an alley behind a tall stone building. Sergeant Barrett lost concentration and ran without checking first. He led us into a group of idle Somalis; they rushed for their weapons. We opened fire but not in time to save Sergeant Barrett. One of the Somalis had let off a burst of fire before he was shot, managing to shoot the sergeant straight in the forehead. Sergeant Barrett dropped to the ground like a rag doll, instantly killed by the shot. The medic went over and took his dog tag "I promise we'll be back for you" he muttered to the corpse of the dead sergeant.

We picked up our things and began to move again, still occasionally surprising enemy soldiers with our unexpected presence. Thousands of armed Somali patrolled Mogadishu and they all wanted our blood. Captain Roberts seemed to have a good idea of where we were going so we let him lead the way through the alleys.

We came to a cluster of dwellings unaware we were walking into a twenty-strong group of resting Somalis. Most were sleeping but a few were patrolling. By the time we realized how deep in we were, we had been spotted by a patrolling soldier. The sound of his AK-47 shooting at us woke the sleeping soldiers. We began to run back trying to escape from the scene whilst most of them were still dazed and confused. The enemy pursued us, pushing us closer and closer to exactly where we didn't want to go, the main road. This would be swarming with Somalis.

"Run and take cover in that building, I'll cover you" Captain Roberts yelled. We ran into a two-story structure that at some point had blown up or collapsed because the roof was caved in on one side leaving metal cables and wires poking out in all directions. I was the last man in so I was to cover the captain whilst he ran in to the building. I waved him in but he was too busy shooting. "Captain, come on!" Once the Captain finished shooting he turned to my direction and shook his head. He loaded a fresh magazine into his gun and ran further down the street to where the Somali were coming from. The captain ducked behind a burnt out car, but by then it was too late for us to help him without being killed.

Now there were only three of us and we had lost the captain. We filed in to one of the rooms in the house. "Where's the captain?" Good asked me.

"He's dead. He died so the Somalis wouldn't know where we are," I replied

"What are we going to do now? What can we do without the captain? He had the radio, he knew the way!"

141

"Calm down Good, we should just wait here until the firing begins to ease and then find the convoy that will be looking for survivors!" The speech from Moore seemed to calm Good from his hysteric state.

We decided to hide in the room we were in, it was on the ground floor so we could go out to flag down the convoy if it came and the room had plenty of cover to hide from the enemy. We were all down to our last few rounds of ammo – we could not afford to get in to another battle.

We waited in that room for about an hour trying to evade being noticed by Somalis who walked past the door or window. Most were too busy talking to each other to pay great attention to the room. We were just about to move out into the street to look for the convoy, when a Somali entered our building. He was walking round patrolling. We all hid, praying he would not come into our room but he did. I was sitting behind an old desk with Moore, and Good was stood against the wall next to the door. The Somali walked in to the room and did not notice any of us. Good sneaked up behind him and drew his knife. He grabbed the Somali over his mouth so he could not shout and ran his knife across his throat. As the Somali dropped to the ground he shot his gun in the struggle. A bullet managed to penetrate the deck and go into Moore's back. Good dropped the now-dead Somali and rushed over to give Moore medical attention.

"Roll him on to his front!" Good said in a hurry. Moore was struggling from the pain and let out a cry. "He's going to die if he doesn't get proper medical attention soon!"

We could now hear more people in the house; all of the noise must have attracted them. All three of us were behind the desk. Me and Good, both clutching our guns. I had my hand over Moore's mouth trying to keep him quiet. The footsteps were fast and nearing our room. The room was stormed with terrifying efficiency. I looked through the hole left from the bullet that hit Moore to see two American soldiers. "Wait, help" I called out to them.

"Sir we got survivors, in the building" they said as they talked into their radios on their collars. Lieutenant Colonel Gary Harrell stepped into the room with his usual casualness about him "You're not going to kill many men down there." He said as he lifted me up "When we heard that gun fire we knew it had to be you."

We were loaded into the Humvees and made our way back to base, we were found just in time as we found out Moore wouldn't have survived much longer without medical attention.

It is said that only the dead see the end of war. I re-live what happened on that day every moment of my life and think about the men who died for me. I tell this story for them.

Matthew Steel

The Crucible

John Proctor's Elegy

My life was spent in harsh, endless toil,
All my wealth was earned through the soil,
I forgot to spend time protecting my soul,
Allowed sin to corrupt my righteous role.
On earth I vowed to cherish my family
Yet I abandoned their wellbeing for the sin of lechery.
In false smiles and flirtatious talk
I left the path I was meant to walk.
The path only trodden by the pure of heart,
That Elizabeth and Goody Nurse would never depart.
I, through vanity and selfish desire,
Prepared myself for Satan's hellfire,
I filled my days with falsehood and sin,
Forsaking the goodness I had grown in.
Now as I am about to die,
The clear light of God is in my eye.
I know it's wrong to lie and cheat,
No longer seduced by a wicked heat.
I feel the purity of my love for my wife
And now accept the end of life.
I die a man forged through fire
Proud of my name now I'm no longer a liar.
I face my fate with head held high,
Knowing my sons will not live a lie.

Elizabeth Allan

The World of Night

A pet to the devil
Was what she'd become.
Her innocence shattered,
Unravelled, undone.
A poisoned apple
(The serpent tempts Eve),
But with a single bite
Inner sin starts to weave
Into the heart of every little lamb
And the farther he draws her
The more she realizes –
It's naught but a sham.
Deeper and deeper she falls,
Whilst he watches with glee.
The eyes of a demon –
That's all she can see.
He marks her for his own, –
Her soul sad away.
Heaven's gates closing –
She will never see day.
Darker and darker –
Her being now tainted.
Hatred, possession –
In the picture he's painted.
Night, (there is no longer day),
Light, (it's been taken away).
Biting into her flesh

He consumes –
Every inch of her humanity.
(Over her he looms)
Like a shadow,
Lying in wait
A voice of poisoned honey –
That was his bait.
Biting into his sin
She fell from the light
Only now knowing
His world of night.

Samantha Smith

John Proctor

As I am about to die,
I can finally hold my head high.

Abigail is the key to my doom,
She entered my soul like an empty room.

In there she found false pride in a name,
A man who sinned yet felt no shame.

I cheated on my innocent wife,
Slicing through her heart with a knife.

In the fortress of my soul was a chink,
Evil entered like Satan's drink.

It flooded through the goodness left,
Drowning my love, leaving Elizabeth bereft.

Witches corrupt if free to roam
Allowed by good men staying at home

One day I awoke to the ills I caused,
An attempt at salvation left me behind locked doors.

My wife would sacrifice her immortal soul.
To save my worthless, lying soul.

At last I saw in a blinding light,
The truth hidden from my blinkered sight.

True love is quiet, brave and pure,
Of Elizabeth alone can I be sure.

My name is worthless if the man remains
A damaged man admitting false claims.

Behold John Proctor mount the scaffold
At peace with Elizabeth's heart to hold.

Leaving sons the memory of a brave man,
Who returned from sin, so anyone can.

I now feel free to meet my fate,
Proudly dying for my families sake.

Mambwe Chella

John Proctor's Last Words

My sons remember me as you grow,
Your mother's love will keep you whole.
I was a man, who sometimes strayed,
And didn't live up to the words I prayed.
I knew my commandments, was a covenanted Christian,
Yet I didn't obey the laws I believed in.
When surrounded by spite and malicious hate
I only did the right thing when it was too late.
In the end I chose to die for my name,
To avoid you growing up in shame.
So please my sons when you remember me,
Truth and goodness are the key,
For a happy life and noble name
Always do what will cause no shame.

Joe Moore

'There is some good in John Proctor'

A harlot's kiss led me astray,
Bold bravado attacked my soul.
I allowed the Devil to walk
Through the hearts and souls of Salem's streets.
Once the hatred and jealousy awoke in their hearts,
Nothing could stop the power of evil,
But me, a lonely sinner
Hiding in the darkness of my lechery.
Wickedness feeding on hypocritical prayers.
What is the good of false worship,
If the hearts are brim-full of sin?
I unleashed years of hidden hatred
By my passionate, unbridled lust.
Cowardly allowing the pure to die
Just to save my false good name
But now at the hour of my death
I finally feel some proper pride.
For in this life I have learnt the truth
That breathing does not amount to much.
If the heart is not true,
I die knowing finally there is some good
In John Proctor.

Harry Attridge

The Sun Rises on my Grieving Heart

The sun rises on my grieving heart
Endless prayers through the night,
The long darkness I yearn to end,
The fate I have resisted,
Refused,
Abhorred,
Is here.
I am the sacrificial lamb
Who has failed in the eyes of God.
My soul was lent to dark forces
Hidden to me in arrogance
Pride
Smug conceit.
The things I valued were not true,
Gratification was my delight
Humility was met by my scorn
True goodness cruelly rejected,
Abandoned
Discarded.
Now in the clear morning light,
I finally see what sin blinded me to,
That I should aspire to,
The pure soul of my wife
Untainted
Unsullied.
Our Love will live on in our children's souls
Uncorrupted by a stain on the family's name.
Remembering with just pride a loving father
Who died to protect their innocent hearts
From my sin.

Nicole Glennon

Inspired by
Shakespeare

Malvolio's Diary

17th July

I cannot believe their nerve. They shout, scream, sing, dance, all in the middle of the night! They must be mad to gabble like tinkers when all is quiet, dark and still. How dare they make an ale house of my lady's house, when they are living at her expense? I knew, and still know, that my lady disapproves of such drunkenness, so what did I do? I went down there to sort them out.

Down I went, into that damp, cold cellar. The floor tiles were so cold I could feel my toes going blue. I almost slipped in a puddle of spilt ale; it stuck to my feet and slithered right between my toes. I distinctly remember shuddering as my foot slipped in that icy puddle. If I hadn't been clutching the banister I would have toppled down those wretched stairs and landed in a heap at Sir Toby's feet. Goodness knows what would have happened if I hadn't caught myself in time. Luckily, Sir Toby and his foolish friends didn't hear a thing, so I righted myself and continued my descent.

They only noticed me when I finally reached their filthy abode. The table in the centre of the room was creaking with the weight of so many tankards. There were little puddles of cheap ale scattered everywhere, being soaked up by the rotten straw that served as a carpet. Sir Toby, Sir Andrew, Maria and Feste were all swigging stale ale laughing and shouting as they gulped down the vile liquid. It's obvious they fear me, for when I appeared, silence reigned over the room. The fools just stared at me, as if I was some sort of apparition or ghost. So I got cracking at them, letting them have a piece of my mind Their drunkenness had reached such a point, that all they did was burst into song, mocking me. Then, Sir Toby comes up to me and calls me nothing but a steward I was so outraged I stormed out of the room and up the stairs. There is no reply anyone can give to such an insult. I could hear them laughing as I marched up the stairs and slammed the door, plunging them into darkness.

Make no mistake, my lady shall hear of this. If she sees sense she might even throw him out. That would teach the ungrateful pig!

18th July

This morning was so beautiful. The sun was shining, the birds were singing, and the garden was filled with golden-yellow sunlight. It was wonderful to be strolling out there, with that gentle breeze brushing over my face. Such wonders of nature made me think of my lady, the fair Olivia. I wondered if my lady would love me, and if she ever did, would she love me with passion? I contemplated some more, and began thinking that if she would love me, she would dream of my good looks. The more I thought, the more it seemed possible, if not probable, that my lady loved me. "After all," I pondered to myself, "she treats me with a more exalted respect than anyone else who serves her."

The morning seemed so perfect, so unspoilt, that I started fantasizing. "To be Count Malvolio." I proclaimed aloud, getting buried in my wild hopes and dreams. "Sitting in my state, calling my officers about me." I sat down on a hard, stone bench, imagining it to be a throne. I continued my one-man performance. "Cousin Toby." I smiled down at a stunted box tree, which was struggling in vain to stay alive. I waggled a finger at it, saying calmly "You must amend your drunkenness." Anyone watching me would have thought I was stark-raving bonkers, but I didn't care. I was in my own world, where no one would laugh, sneer or snigger. "Besides, you spend the treasure of your time with a foolish knight." I smiled some more at the box tree, as if it were a small child. "Sir Andrew does you no good." I could see Sir Toby, right there in my mind's eye, looking extremely embarrassed, then crawling away, muttering "Yes my Lord."

It was utter bliss for me then, with the image of Sir Toby fresh in my mind.

I heard a subtle crunch of footsteps, so I looked up. I saw nothing, so I turned my attention back to the box tree. It was then that I noticed the letter, inches from my feet. I bent down to pick it up. The letter was light, small and dainty, almost feminine. I turned it over and was surprised to find my lady's hand. It was sealed with the impressure of Lucrece, which only my lady uses. I was so excited I could barely sit still. The envelope read 'To the unknown beloved, this, and my good wishes.' Gingerly, I slid my finger under the red wax seal, and took out the letter with the utmost care. It was folded neatly into a rectangle, as my lady always does before she slides the letter into the envelope. My hands were trembling as I began to read quietly to myself:

Love knows I love;
But who?
Lips, do not move,
No man must know'

I paused to steady my shaking hands. Could she have written this letter to me? I had to find out.

'I may command where I adore,
But silence, like a Lucrece knife,
With bloodless stroke my heart doth gore,
M.O.A. I. doth sway my life.'

But who was M.O.A.I? I had never heard of such a man.
Then it struck me: M began my name, M for Malvolio.
"But it should be A next" My hope had begun to fade when
I finally figured the puzzle out. Every one of those letters
appears in my name. It was true! My lady loved me! I
almost leapt with joy, but stopped myself just in time;
just in case any man should pass by. I continued reading
hurriedy:

'If this fall into thy hand, revolve. In my stars I am above
thee, but be not afraid of greatness. Some are born great,
some achieve greatness, and some have greatness thrust
upon them. Be opposite with kinsmen, surly with servants.
Remember who commended thy yellow stockings, and
wished to see thee ever cross gartered. If thou entertain'st
my love, let it appear in thy smiling, thy smiles become
thee well.'

I could feel myself smiling like a maniac as I forgot all
dignity and shouted to the world "Jove, I thank thee! I
will smile, I will do everything that thou wilt have me."
Then, remembering her dainty words 'No man must know'
I quickly straightened myself and continued on my walk,
with a joyful smile plastered on my face.

I will smile for her, with all my joy. Oh, how I have been
longing to parade that pair of yellow stockings I got for
Christmas some years ago.

I was so overjoyed. My lady loved me! She had even written
a letter to me portraying her love. So I was extremely glad

when she sent for me this afternoon. I saw it as a great opportunity to show her my love. When Maria came for me I was all ready; I had quickly pulled on my yellow stockings and cross-gartered them as soon as I returned from my walk. She gave me a funny look, but I haven't a clue why. Any fellow is allowed to smile, especially when they're in love.

Olivia greeted me as she always did; I presumed she didn't want to give the game away to Maria. I couldn't wait until my lady dismissed Maria and we would be alone. 'I might even propose to her' I thought to myself as I replied.

"Sweet lady, ho, ho!" To my surprise my lady looked more puzzled than delighted. She glanced down at my stockings, and I saw her face go pale. I was shocked. She had told me to come smiling to her, and always wear my gorgeous yellow silk stockings cross-gartered. After a while staring at me, she replied in a shaky tone;

"Smil'st thou? I sent for thee upon a sad occasion." I was even more bemused. She loved me; she should be overjoyed that I'd come to her. Why was it a sad occasion? I expressed my feelings rather brashly to her then, forgetting Maria completely.

"Sad, lady?" I smiled at her, and tilted my head in a rather boyish way. "I could be sad: this does make obstruction in the blood, this cross-gartering." My lady seemed aghast. She stared, with disgust at my wonderful cross-gartered yellow stockings, as if they bore some awful contagious disease. She looked up at me with those beautiful emerald green eyes, and my heart almost melted. 'She must just be pretending in case Maria should suspect our love' I reassured myself. How could she not adore my marvellous yellow stockings? But still, in the back of my mind, I couldn't help thinking that there was something wrong. These feelings were only increased when she gave me her reply.

"Why, how dost thou, man? What is the matter with thee?" I kept smiling, putting those doubtful feelings behind: She loved me, I was sure of it, and there was no point in worrying myself.

"Not black in my mind, though yellow in my legs. It did come to his hands, and commands shall be executed." My lady started looking at me as if I were mad.

"Wilt thou go to bed, Malvolio?" There was my chance. She was obviously ready to go all the way, while trying to fool Maria into thinking I was mad. I could have kissed her right there and then, but I restrained myself, playing along with her bravado. I wanted to hit myself, for having any doubts that she didn't love me. So as to fool Maria even more, I whispered my next comment in my lady's ear, hoping she would dismiss Maria and we could be alone.

"To bed? Ay, sweetheart, and I'll come to thee." I took her dainty hand and kissed it gently to indicate my point. She pulled it away sharply, but I knew it was only to delude Maria.

"God comfort thee! Why dost thou smile so, and kiss my hand so oft?" I winked at her as Maria spoke.

"How do you, Malvolio?" We had her fooled! My lady and I had convinced Maria I was mad, and I could court Olivia without any suspicion. But remembering the letter, I decided to carry my lady's final request: to be surly with servants. I swelled with pride as I replied to Maria, treating her as she was, a mere servant.

"At your request? Yes, nightingales answer daws!" I had

really got her then, and I was enjoying myself. It was good to pay her back for the incident the previous night. But she wasn't going to accept my comments. Oh no, she sided with my lady yet again, convinced I was mad and my lady wanted to be rid of me.

"Why appear you with this ridiculous boldness before my lady?" I couldn't be bothered to answer her, so I turned to my lady once more.

"Some are born great." My lady laughed, realising I was reciting her very words.

"Some achieve greatness, and some have greatness thrust upon them."

"Heaven restore thee!" exclaimed my lady, obviously overjoyed that I'd remembered her grand speech.

"Go to, thou art made, if thou desir'st to be so." I was enjoying acting out her very words; it was fun, and Maria would not have a clue what we were talking about. "Am I made? Why this is very midsummer madness!" proclaimed my lady.

A servant came in and informed my lady that Orsino's man had arrived. I was just about to be surly to the servant again when he left to fetch Cesario. I was aghast when I heard my lady saying "good Maria, let this fellow be looked to, where's my cousin Toby? Let some of my people have a special care of him, I would not have him miscarry for the half of my dowry." I was horrified, she was supposed to send Maria out, but not to fetch Sir Toby. Maybe I had overdone her instructions? Maybe she really did think I was mad. I didn't know what to do, so I just stood there like a fool waiting for Sir Toby to come and mock me.

Sir Toby came in shouting at the top of his voice like a maniac, even more than I had done.

"Which way is he, in the name of Sanctity? If all the devils of hell be drawn in little, and legion possessed him, yet I'll speak to him." I couldn't be bothered with the scum, so after some bickering and me shouting. 'Go off, I discard you. Let me enjoy my private. Go off' I was finally allowed to go free.

How dare they treat me like I was a madman, possessed by the devil himself? I knew they were scheming something. They wanted to take my water to a wise woman! What good would that do? Anyway, God knows I am not mad, and so do I. I am glad I know the truth: my lady loves me, and we have duped everyone else into thinking I was mad. That way, I will surely be allowed to see my lady.

20th July

Yesterday was pure hell. They came for me in the night, trussed me up, and threw me in this dump! There is no light, no food, and no water! Just cold, hideous darkness, eating away at my mind. I don't know what to do. My lady loves me, why has she locked me away? I feel cheated, tricked, abused, betrayed. I am not mad, I am not mad, I AM NOT MAD! Why does no one come? The only soul I have seen for two days is Sir Topaz the curate, a mean, unkind man. He denied me everything I asked, he would not even go to my lady! He told me there were bay windows, with sunlight streaming in. He is the lunatic, not me! I suppose I must count myself lucky that I was passed ink and paper by that fool, Feste. Otherwise I wouldn't even be able to write.

Oh, curses. I smudged it again. This paper will be unreadable by the time I'm finished with it. If only Feste had brought my diary, then I would be able to laugh at the smart comments I made, and forget the awful cave I'm stuck in. The shadows creep around me like strange ghosts. I can hear the eerie sound of water dripping through the rocks all around me. This horrific cell is enough to drive any man mad. When will I get out of here?

Claire Westrop

Lear

Wind howls, lightening flashes
Illuminating the withered face
Once a monarch, ruling all he could see
Now trapped by the elements
Surrounded by chaos.
The turmoil of a mind decaying
An aging body, a sagging brain.
No help and comfort from own blood,
Hidden help from friends scorned.
The faithful Fool, a wise councillor,
Finding shelter from the whips
Of rain, of wind, of heartbreak.
Under the madness lies a soul
Who led himself to his own doom.
He spurned a truly loving daughter,
Seduced by the flattery of greedy voices,
Seduced by the knowledge of a shallow heart.
Wind screams, rain pounds
Thunder wrecks an old man's dreams.
As the memory dies, the shadow remains
Of a King once revered, now shamed.

Abigail Dally

Gloucester

O I have lost my sight
My two eyes are gone
Simply because I am loyal and true.
My wicked son Edmund
May it be done to you
To suffer as I have
What have I done ?
To deserve such treatment from my child.
I have nothing else to live for,
How I wish this dark life could end.

Mambwe Chella

Lear

Once I ruled this vast Kingdom,
My daughters cherished their noble father,
They cared for my every need,
Lavishing their love on my aging head.
I tired of the labour as my body slowed,
And felt the time was ripe
To pass my power and Kingdom
Into the loyal hands of loving daughters.
But how was I to tell the truth
When masked by smiles and gentle caresses.
Stony hearts, ambitious minds.
Venom.
Two cruelly disposed of an empty King,
Having given all to their rapacious hands,
I too disposed of a true heart,
Sending Cordelia across the cold channel,
Slicing through her loving heart,
To give her birthright away to sisters
Whose loyalty lay only with themselves.
Soon the Kingdom resembled my shattered heart
As brother fouled brother and sisters plotted.
As I lie here dying a broken man,
At last I know the truth behind the smiles.
Simple words are true and faithful
Flattery hides the evil intent.
Look not on smiles and chilly eyes
But on love given over many years,
And my sweet Cordelia now lies dead in my arms
The last embrace of my true daughter.

Chris Barrett

Goneril

The old man does not realize
His madness, others greed,
The years have locked him away
Never to be freed.

Mine own sister
She has taken my man
Edmund, Oh Edmund
Join me in my destructive plan

Regan might have golden hair,
Her soul, her mind is base
So evil, so cruel, crushing
Love is a trait you'll never find.

To poison her tongue
Just to hinder her life
Edmund, the kingdom will be mine
As your wife together we'll rule.

Once the pretty one is hanged
And the old man is dead –
I have poisoned my dear sister –
I will live, I will rule, I will love

Melanie Hayden

Lear

Survey the damaged land,
Ripped apart by family feuds
Sisters' greed and fearsome anger
Leading to cold cruelty.
An old, mad King
Foolish and exposed,
Three daughters grown
Two ambitious, one loving
Insanity judges flattery true
And abandons a kingdom to harpies.
The damage grows as a harvest
Of wicked weeds and grotesque greed.
Old, alone in a wild storm
Loyal Fool with wise advice
And men disguised
Who must hide their faces,
Fearing punishment –
Loyalty and truth
Hounded from this land.
Only cruelty grows
In this damaged land.

Conor FitzPatrick

Nothing

Nothing; the word that got me banished,
The word that could not mean anything
But it meant everything.
I loved my father because he was king
I did not love the king because he was my father.
The foolish game's gone wrong
Because the winner did not win.
Goneril, our eldest born, speak first.
The flattery begins.
Goneril gets the first chance as usual,
A chance to win her father's heart that she will never be able to take.
No matter what comes out of the eldest born's mouth
The game she plays cannot be won by words
So now it's my turn, my turn to lie,
My chance to tell a naïve man what he wants to hear,
For what is mine already.
I shall not participate in lying and cheating,
I will tell the truth, speak my mind
And still win.
Nothing my lord.
He repeats my word to give me another chance to humour him.
I repeat to him what he fears...nothing.
Nothing will come of nothing. Speak again.
The king does not understand the love I have for him
Something I felt I could not lie about or dress up.
The King's advisor sees what is correct
He protests to his master the sense he should see.
A brave man and ally to my cause of justice,
Where principles count for more than hollow flattery.
If I love my father with my whole heart what do I have left to
Love my future husband with?

Joe Harry

Cordelia's Soliloquy

Declare my love?
But what for? I have nothing to prove;
I acknowledge his presence,
With great love and care.
I love my father as he loves me,
He knows of this, Goneril simply cannot compare
To this.
Her only desires are to feed,
Her green demons. Pure evil is what I see,
Only one thing in mind she does have.
Typical of my sisters to fulfil my father's desires without
A care in the world. They do not
Love our father as they say.
All their love is entangled between their lusts and
Fake faces.

But wait, express my love! He wants
This of me?
It's as if he needs the reassurance, the sort of
Certainty of my love.
It is not right, I cannot declare
My love.

I love thee with all my heart;
But words,
No amount of words that
Fall off my tongue,
Will satisfy thy father's wishes.
He has seen my actions, he watched me grow
Fonder of him.
I have fully returned my love
With great honour.
No more can be done; if this is what he wants,
A foolish game
To unveil our darker sides
Then I am not one to take part.

I do not feel obliged to respond with some lies.
If this is what he wants then I shall
Be first to object.

Nothing.
That is all that will escape from my lips.
Not more, nor less.
Nothing, I know, will not please my father,
It will kick start his brain and send
Adrenalin to all the cells in his body.
Anger, frustration, rage is all that is displayed
Upon his wrinkled face.

Banished he says.
Disowned, I am ridiculed and cursed
In front of all.
But fractured my heart is not; he has mistaken
My words.
He cannot see the immaturity of his way.
Why such fury at such little speech?
I simply cannot
Fit together my love.
It is something far more complicated and deep,
Which cannot
Be compared to a meaningless quantity of land.
I pity his arrogance, the corruption he has
Caused within our relationship.
He has stubbornly not thought about his selfish
Actions, and has put strain on my love for him.

Nicole Smith

Cordelia

Regal and bigheaded
These two words sum up my father.
He needed a huge gold plated palace just to house his ego.

The money that he spent on this palace.
The diamond and crystal embellished chandeliers that he
imported from St. Petersburg;
It took over four hundred people just to make one for him.

We entered, there he was, seated on his throne, sceptre in one
hand; orb in the other.
His yes-men gathered around him looking for something else
to gossip about.
Well, I will be giving them something.

The kingdom would be divided, but the way that the
opinionated bigot chose was
Terrible.
Being asked to tell your father how much you love him, in the
most opulent way possible, left me very annoyed.
He was almost a shadow father to me anyway, he never
actually looked after me,
His loyal servants did that.

My two sisters married off to rich dukes, they don't love
them, they just married for the money.
They now have something else to brag about at the palace
soirées.
They just want another item on their lists to tell their
blueblood friends.

The chandeliers reflected him as if they were three giant
mirrors.
Maybe this is why he had them made, so that he could see
himself ten times
His actual size.

Goneril and Regan were standing there.
He was choosing us in chronological order.
They prepared their false malevolent speeches.

Yes it is an easy task but for what purpose?
More flattery for the king that was the purpose.
Goneril could easily produce an amazing sonnet of verse to
put forward to the king.
Then the duke would be happy; more land for the estate.

She spoke and he adored it; that was her third of the estate.
He was beginning to feel very regal and empowered now.
He was floating in the clouds above the hierarchy pyramid in
his mind.

Regan stepped forward another third disappeared.

The noise in the hall was deafening.
The discussion between the king and his senate was
reverberating around the room.
The crystals on the chandeliers began to sway, the king's
clothes were faded and discoloured.
Much like the fading of his grasp on this country.

Kent began to speak, someone was on my side of the
argument.
The words he spoke were true, my father with his delusions of
grandeur just
Passed him by and carried on.

Kent's words left me with hope.
I knew that they would end up as shelter in this storm.

My father was gaining insanity very quickly.
I know that the only thing that I can do is get as far away
from him as possible.
Before he forces me into exile I will go of my own accord.

Adam Jankowski

'Love and be silent...'

Declare our love,
But what for?
What is his twisted mind
Devising now?
Of course, she will flatter hium,
With a million false cries.
She will jump,
As far as is needed.
She will run,
As fast as is asked.
For land or a fortune.
Goneril has set her whole life aside,
Fulfilling father's needs.
And what for?
What good or happiness
Has come from it?
Yes, she is wealthy,
But she is dejected.
She is in a marriage with no love,
Nor trust or loyalty.
What is life without love,
An honest love?
Yes our relationship was once
Sister-like,
But that was abolished,
Through the choices she made.
And to lower herself, once again
To play his foolish games,
Is beyond my understanding.
Perhaps this however
Is not lowering herself.
Perhaps she has reached the
Lowest point possible.

Express my love!
Has he not listened
For all this time?

I am not like Goneril,
I am not like Regan.
My loyalties stand, and I
Shall stand right beside them.
I love my father and sisters,
As much is as is needed,
As much as a person should love them.
But I love my father
As he is my father, not
Because he is the King.
I do not believe in playing games,
Especially when the final prize,
Is either land or money.
I have repaid
Through love. But I
Shall never let someone change
Who I am.
Does he not trust me?
Is this all for reassurance
That I still love him.
He loves me with all his heart.
It is known by the whole land.
And I give him my love back.
But I do not give him my
Heart.
It is for me
And whoever destiny brings me.
I will flatter my father.
No words,
No lies,
Will satisfy my father.

My father's a strong man.
Built on character and power.
But a weakness in him,
That can be seen from
A million miles away,
Is that of betrayal.
Or being told he is wrong.

To have someone disagree
With what he says
And speak up for what they believe in,
Would tear him apart.
Until this point,
It has only ever been me
That stood up to my father.
Myself and the fool.
The only people to not rise
To the childish games being played.
Not Kent,
Never have I imagined
Kent to be the person to
Side with me,
Tell my father what he
Has done is wrong.
He sounded so serious,
So relieved,
As if he had wanted to
Speak up to my father
For ages.

My father looked defeated.
And although I should also
Feel defeated when my
Father does, I did not.
I felt joyous.
Flattered that Kent was
Sticking up for me.
I felt a tinge of
Confidence rushing
Through me.
Maybe this is the break.
The big break to
Destroy my father.

Kirsty Harkness

Imagine

Just a Thought

Open water
Blank canvas
Free to whatever ideas are welcome,
Nothing is unreachable,
You are on your own cloud nine.

Glazed eyes,
Vacant expression,
Only concentrating on your own world,
Far, far away,
Where no one else can find you.

High up in a cloud,
Down low in the dirt,
Anywhere you want to go,
Alone,
Or in a sea of people,

In a horror,
Or a dream,
Feeling safe, unwatched,
Unguarded,
In a fairy tale,

Feeling captured,
In your own self,
Until you are rescued,
And you can escape to reality, freedom,
If you can call yourself free.

Leanne Searle

Vaizduotė

Vaizduotė - platus laukas,
Žalias miškas matos toli.
Žalios mintys kartais atslinksta,
Bet mašiniukas ir Vėl jau kely.

Aukšti medžiai – seni ąžuolai.
Nauji lapai. Seni – pakelėj.
Vidurnaktį šiečia žvaigždute viena;
Lininiai laukai ir sena Lietuva...

Bet kažkas čia ne taip,
Man nereikia čia būt.
Aš užvedu mersą,
Atgal reikia dūkt.

Staiga aš sustoju.
Dairausi aplink...
Diena tartum paukštė
Nakties skrenda link.

Ir štai aš suvokiu –
Tai sapnas tiktai.
Vaizduotė tai laukas,
Jame – ąžuolai...

Veronika Nekrasova

Imagination

Imagination – wide field.
Far away you can see a green forest.
Green thoughts sometimes creep up.
But a car is on the road again.

Tall trees – old oak trees.
New leaves. Old ones in the gutter.
A single star shines in the middle of the night.
Flax fields and old Lithuania.

But something's wrong here,
I'm not supposed to be here.
I step on the gas
I have to rush back.

Suddenly I stop,
Look around...
Day like a bird,
Flies towards night.

And suddenly I realize –
It's just a dream.
Imagination is a field,
In it – oak trees.

Veronika Nekrasova

The Impossible Meadow

The perfume of lilies gather themselves up into the wind,
The sun is a parrot perched up on a blue canvas,
The meadows of flowers show a stained glass window.
You stare straight through until the eyes focus,
They focus on a large mansion, which gradually spins into the
image of an ink pen,

The ink pen is in your hand,
All you do is stare silently,
And you watch;
You watch as your hand moves constantly across the page.

You are worried and throw the pen,
But to your surprise it does not fall;
You think you're wrong, but the pen,
The pen is now a tennis racket.

You lift yourself from the ground,
And smile as you realize,
That you are playing tennis on the beach,
You miss the ball and spin round.

As you turn, you see,
That the sea is coming close.
Needing more space,
More space for IDEAS!

Jasmine Doyle

Strange

Its brains without hearts.
Have set saint against sinner.
Sprinting into the vortex of the opposites.
Astounding the mother of all strangeness with your entry.
Surprised she is.
But you are not unexpected.

Falling in a downward spiral.
The lights flicker from black to white. As your fantasy becomes reality.

No voice.
No whisper.
Nothing stirs.
The resurrected tower flows into the golden glistening solution.
Amazed at this sight!?

...

this is just the tip of the iceberg!

Tom Davies

Imagery of the Mind

Yellow like the Sahara desert.
The golden sand builds a barren dessert of intelligence.
No liquid is present
Yet the constant whisper of waves lapping over each other rings in your ears and
lulls you to sleep.
They each contain an idea.
A piece to the puzzle.

Constructed like a cocktail, my imagination is layer upon layer of ideas.
The sweet taste of knowledge presses against your lips.
Begging to get in.
Before the gate hole closes.
Yet again.
Once again.

Slowly the chlorine rises like a muggy mist.
Its breaks to the surface of the swimming pool with ease.
As it rises the ideas develop.
And in the end.
The word is spoken.
Yet a mystery to the anticipating audience.

The eagle awakes.
Feeding time again.
Its claws as sharp as hit-man's knife.
Swiftly it soars.
No scream is let out.
Once again the hit-man is victorious.
Without a doubt.
Once again yet again.

The engine roars, the trigger is pulled.
The unique doors slide open in a disorderly fashion.
The ideas click as smooth like the silent Gallarado.
As it glides through the open air.
Illuminating all in its path by its crystallized rims and shiny peach colour scheme.
Like a golden hawk.
Swooping into the black hole of my imagination.

Tom Davies

Does Time Stop?

This moment
Tick-tock goes the clock.
Nothing but hands and a face.
Do where and when really matter?
Of course they do.
Who has done it?
Why?
The sound of the clock is drowned
By the screaming of the sirens.
Time goes by slowly for those who wait.
But she didn't wait;
She ran straight out.
People are frozen
with tears paused
whilst running halfway down their sad faces.
Flowers are lying at the side of the road.
I am the time lord.
I can stop time.
I have stopped it so you can understand.
But maybe you don't.
Some say time flies by.
Some say time stops.
And it did.
The sad thing is, I can stop time
But I can't rewind it.
And time did stop for Amy.
She was only 14.

Katrina McNair

Maybe

He roars
And the jaguar roars
Black as ten pm
Yet nobody hears
Atop the highest mountain
He roars
Yet nobody hears
Maybe their ears are blocked
Maybe they must hear with their eyes
Maybe
Maybe

Like the swift
Even when sleeping she is active
Except she is never active
Only hyperactive
Like a toaster
Sucks in ideas
Only to regurgitate them tasting sweeter than before

A ball being kicked around by so many
A ball of the purest platinum
Yet instead of breaking their toes
She kisses their feet
They are stars
Game on

The Veyron whips past
Unique
Twenty four in the world
The faster it goes the more it changes
Penetrated by none
Least the almighty 50 calibre
Its bullets like dust on a titanium wall
Penetrated by none

But maybe it isn't
Maybe it isn't the orange clover in a field of green
Maybe it isn't Robbie the robot
Maybe it is just a computer
Following orders
Occasionally malfunctioning
Maybe
Maybe
But when it is allowed to malfunction
It explodes

Sam Sheldon

Nightmare

A nightmare
One that won't end
Replaying
Constantly in your mind
Like a broken record
Stuck
On the same 3 seconds
Over
And over
Drumming into your mind
Clawing at your skin
Its fingertips pulling
As if to rub away your mask
So,
All that is left
Is what you once were
The true you
The one that is scared
Scared of what happened
Scared of what may happen
Scared to be yourself
Scared
Just scared

That night
Those events
Imprinted into
Your brain
Your heart
Your soul
You can't escape
Its grip
You can't escape
Its consequences
The things you did
The things you regret
The way you feel
You can't be yourself

Stuck behind that mask
The false smiles
Hiding those tears
On your placid face
Like a frightened child
You hide
Behind anything you can
Like a rose blowing in the wind
You go with whatever
Everyone else wants to do
Anything
just as long as
You're invisible
Like the faded ink in an old diary
Snow melting in the sun

You'll never shake off
Those memories
Those tears
They'll just keep coming
Until
All that is left of you
Is
A shadow
A shadow of your former self
You'll just keep
Disappearing inside
Until
It becomes too much
You'll end up going insane
The same thing going
round
And round

Your head
You'll end up screaming
Screaming because
you can't control who you are any longer
Screaming because you know
You shouldn't have done it

But,
If you knew that
Then why?
Why did you do it?
How could you have the conscience you do that?
Because now
You will never be able
To escape those memories
Your nightmare won't ever end
Close your eyes
All you will see is
What you have done
The knife
Cutting deep
Blood
The screams
Despair
Pain
Betrayal.
How you were able
To kill
Jealousy consumed
Your every fibre of being
Like a cloak of evil drawing you in
Just because,
Her shadow didn't pull her away from
What was going on
And what she really was
Wasn't a decent motive
But it isn't me that has
To live
With
The screams
It isn't me that has to live with the nightmare...

Katy Gearing

Like an Attentive Pupil, Imagination Prowls

Bursting to a ferocious start with the speed of a Ferrari and the strength
of a Tornado,
Flying as free as an eagle soaring through boundless skies,
Soft as pure white silk and yet as strong as titanium,
Unfathomable like the depths of the sea and yet as skilled as a master
sportsman,
With the tenderness of a violin and the power of a tank.
Imagination prowls.

Standing tall and proud like a majestic oak,
Seeing all like a camera atop a top hat in a card game,
Swimming through the depths of possibility like a whale through a new-
found ocean,
At home in its exploration of possibilities
Like an attentive pupil,
Imagination roves and learns.

Imagination, a creation that was imagined and yet an imagination that
creates.
Like a computer, it is easily accessible and has the capability to expand.
Like a sofa, it can be humbled and can adapt to this like water poured from
one cup to another
Imagination masters.

Like a ruby clear cut and set in purest gold,
Like a work of art that is so sensuous you wish to stare upon it for eternity,
Like a photo of a long gone lover
As fine as silk which has been spun from the tears of angels
And as beautiful as a snow-peaked mountain
Imagination is precious.

Consistent as sand falling through an hour glass,
Reliable as a loyal butler,
Resolute like a noble oak tree
Until one day imagination ends as dusk.

Joe Seward

Imagination

The imagination has the power to transform off road and on road
Forever changing to suit weathers undergoing a tropical storm.
Subtle as a seed but ferocious by its bloom,
The sunflower detonates a delightful heat
As does the sun lighting the head of each and every person
Spreading delight.
Tastes of summer liquids, cool, fresh, sensational flavours
Its cool down is ice cold as a church stone floor
Sheltered away from the summer blaze.
The tall glass windows stand triumphant
Reflecting colours of the rainbow
Energized by the sun
Yet subtle enough to be seen.

Full of wonder
The imagination hypnotizes the mind into a deep daydream.
Awoken by the pressure of sinking into failure
The steel hull effectively holds her above the winding waves
In place of a safety barrier
That protects all from trespassing into danger
Emphasizing the consequences of a cliff edge.

Miles down there is a whole world to be seen and heard;
Sandcastles housing mindboggling creatures
Endangered by the child, the pet dog and the salt spray of the sea.
Its shape changes from place to place
Image to image.
Shadowing over the gritty sand
The tall wise palm tree stands.
Then, by surprise, the robin red-breast may catch your eye
With its rouge tummy, stern and bold, then flutters to a new idea.
That new idea is a material,
Silky cool, a sarong
Gentle to touch.
Then when all has been done for the day
A street lamp turns on to guard the night,
To allow imagination to run.

Lucy Mills

If death is the loser and life is the winner

If death is the loser and life is the winner
Then the world is bright
Only beams of light
Only smiles
For miles
For miles
But what
But not
No death no problems
No death no life
No yin no yang
Nothing
Right to die or duty to
Duty to live or right to

If life is the loser and death is the winner
Eternal darkness
All inky black
Or
Maybe
All trees of green
Skies of blue
A world of yours
A world of ours
No sinners nor saints
None in the middle too
Just me and you
And you
And you

Sam Sheldon

Let's Touch the Sky

Let's touch the sky; escape from reality
Soar through the clouds, soar through the trees.
If life never ends and death never starts,
(And each bad day is forgot)
– Be living the dream

Leaving our sadness and our sorrow (and the goodbyes,
lies and tries) towards the everlasting glow
Let's touch the sky, without a doubt,
Nor a fear dwelling in our past,
Behold the moment, the here and the now
(The end is always near, the end is always near)
– Be living the dream

Without a glimpse or a glance or a look to the
forgotten, towards the everlasting glow

Let's touch the sky; together we will
We'll be forever, living in the moment (now and forever)
We'll touch the sky,
Together we'll touch the sky

Leanne Searle

Printed in the United Kingdom
by Lightning Source UK Ltd.
131943UK00002B/70-153/P